TWENTY YEARS
DEAD

RICHARD FARREN BARBER

Let the world know:
#IGotMyCLPBook!

Crystal Lake Publishing
www.CrystalLakePub.com

WELCOME
TO ANOTHER

CRYSTAL LAKE PUBLISHING
CREATION

CHAPTER 1

FOR THE FINAL three miles of the journey, headlights flashed across the vegetation as the truck lurched between potholes. More than once, David saw silvered eyes staring out from the undergrowth. Just wild animals, but his imagination played tricks and created enough monsters to fill his nightmares for the next decade. He was beyond tired; a full day in the classroom followed by a hundred-mile drive on cruddy roads had ground him to dust.

The steering wheel bucked under his hands, and he had to grip hard just to keep on the road. He slowed to a crawl to avoid slamming into one of the gnarled trees that lined both sides of the route.

"They could have put it somewhere more accessible," Helen said.

He didn't have the chance to respond before they hit a deep pothole and the truck dropped a couple of inches, like falling into a trough on a wild sea. Something in the back of the truck made a loud metallic clang and he prayed it was just a loose tool slamming onto the flatbed.

But that was a worry for later, now he just needed to get to the damned graveyard in one piece. A light up

1

ahead flickered on and off like a lighthouse. It probably had nothing to do with the cemetery, but David hung on to the knowledge that the journey was nearly over.

The truck groaned, creaking with each motion. Helen put her hands on the dashboard to steady herself.

"There it is," she said.

David had been expecting it for ten minutes; ever since the SatNav had told him, 'Your destination is on the right,' and the screen had shown a large patch of nothing for miles around. The sign was tucked away by the side of the road, obscured by tree branches and overgrown briars that wound across the faded lettering.

Welcome to Gilroes Cemetery

His arms ached from battling the road for the last couple of miles and he push-pulled the steering wheel in a wide circle to turn the truck through the gap in the trees. The headlamps picked up a gravel surface with missing chunks like moon craters. There was a half dozen vans parked up; rugged trucks and Landrovers covered in scratches and mud. Working vehicles unlike the SUVs and pristine All Terrain jeeps he saw flitting from one shop to the next back home.

He felt the need to say something. "We're here at last," he announced as he steered across the ground to park in a rough line with the other cars.

"You must be knackered."

He turned off the ignition and listened to the tick-tick-tick of the engine as it cooled down. He turned off the headlights. With the moon obscured by clouds, a sea of night pooled up against the windscreen.

The seat creaked as Helen leaned forward. He

waited for her to say how creepy the place was, but she was silent. He heard her breathing.

Something moved off to David's left, but whatever was out there had already gone by the time he turned to look. He felt, rather than saw, a shape slip further into the darkness.

The drive out to the cemetery reminded him of childhood journeys sandwiched between his two aunts admonishing him to sit still. Finally, his mother would turn around and simply say, "David." No explanation. No demand. Just his name, spoken in a stern tone, but that was enough.

Nearly twenty years later he could feel the ghosts of Jean and Martel in the truck with him, and he was seven years old once more. He didn't try to explain it to Helen. She wouldn't understand.

He grabbed the torch from the pocket of the door and stepped down from the truck. He paused beside one of the Landrovers. There was a discreet decal on the back window: Matthew Johnson. Family Director. 07700 900 678. He assumed if he checked the next vehicle he would find another small sticker to identify the owner was also a professional.

The car park was at the base of an amphitheatre, where the surrounding hills were studded with gravestones. In the fading light, the only landmarks were the small burning torches which David assumed belonged to Family Directors set up beside their plots.

The cemetery was different to how he remembered. It felt compressed as if the graves were piled on top of him. His vision was limited to the first few rows of graves—the oldest part of the cemetery where the names had eroded from the gravestones. He walked past these first graves, conscious that his fear that a hand might reach up from the ground and seize hold of his ankle was based purely on too many hours watching hokey horror films and bad documentaries. That didn't happen, not in the old ground.

He went around to the back of the truck where he had loaded a pile of equipment including a chair he'd driven thirty miles to collect: old but solid. He strapped the first rucksack to his back and found a series of ragged steps which wound up between the graves. Helen followed.

"I think it's up on the right," David said. He paused. Nothing looked the same, not the trees or the graves or the surrounding landscape. He moved in that direction before Helen could reply.

When David stopped walking, the footsteps behind him stuttered to a halt. The only sound in the cemetery was the wind rustling through the leaves. Trees overhung the turn-of-the-century graves where faded engraving remembered Edwards and Fredericks and Ethels.

"You didn't have to do this," Helen said. "When my aunt died, my cousins paid for someone to come and sit with her."

"Leeches."

"It's what people do. Professionals know how to speak to the risen. It's just the same as having someone help when your parents are too old to live by themselves."

He wanted to point out that he had never asked her to tag along. That she had insisted on accompanying him, even when he'd made it clear he wanted to go alone.

David surveyed the graveyard. He was fairly

confident his father's grave was somewhere at the back of the plot near the stone wall. He pushed away the guilt which suggested he should know where his dad was buried because he should have come by more often over the last twenty years, but it was a 200-mile round trip that had never become a habit.

Maybe when all of this was done he would make a point of returning to pay his respects properly. He would come every month and tidy the grave, spend a few minutes chatting to his dad. His mother wouldn't like that, but she didn't need to know.

"This way."

"Are you listening to me?" Helen asked.

He stopped and turned to face Helen. "I'm doing this. You can come if you want, or you can stay in the truck, but I'm doing this."

"I was just saying . . . "

He started walking again. A moment later Helen's footsteps followed. He didn't want to argue, not today, but he'd made up his mind about coming to his dad's rising years ago and there was nothing Helen, his mother, or anyone else could say that would change his mind.

Way over in the corner of the graveyard there was movement. In the shadows of the late evening, it was impossible to be certain, but David assumed it was one of the Family Directors. That was okay for other people, but the idea of his dad waking up to be met by a stranger who didn't know him and didn't care about him was obscene. Helen was wrong; it wasn't anything like caring for an ailing parent. The Rising would take a day at most, and once it was over, he could get on with his life and his dad could get on with his death.

As he started up the hill, he heard his breath loud in his ears. Behind him he was aware Helen's spin classes and Yoga were paying off: she still had breath left to talk. "I think it's a bad idea. Your mum thinks it's a bad idea. Why do you always have to make things so difficult for everyone?"

The effort required to climb the hill gave him an excuse not to reply. He didn't have the words to explain why it was important. It was an instinct and that was good enough for him. It should be good enough for Helen, too.

He paused halfway up the hill and looked down. His truck was a smudge of grey in the car park.

"We could be here until tomorrow night."

"I don't mind," Helen said.

"You said it was a waste of time."

"It is, but if you're adamant you're going to do this then I'm staying. I let Mick know I wouldn't be in tomorrow."

"He's okay with that? I thought he was a hardass."

"He likes to think he is, but I haven't asked for time off for a couple of months and I worked extra hours during last month's surge, so he couldn't really complain."

"Thanks." He couldn't see her face properly in the dark so he had to imagine how she might look, her soft brown eyes, her blonde hair. She had a terrible habit of being able to say just the right thing at the right time. Even when she was wrong, she was right.

"I *am* going to do this," he told her.

"I know. I just felt I had to try and persuade you out of it one last time. It's going to be horrible."

"Why?"

Helen's silhouette shrugged. "It just is. I can feel it."

"My dad's going to claw his way out of his grave after twenty years buried in the ground. What could possibly go wrong?" David said.

Helen laughed, soft and respectful within the stillness of the cemetery.

He waited until Helen stepped forward to join him. She placed her hand inside his, and they continued to walk the hill up to his father's grave.

CHAPTER 2

AS THEY ROSE, David began to scan the line of graves. The fear that his dad had already risen gnawed away at him. There was no way he could have got the dates wrong and yet the feeling persisted. Although he was panting from the exertion, he was almost running. Most of the plots were pools of darkness, but the occasional hollow indentations in front of tilted headstones were sufficient to encourage David to go faster.

"Slow down," Helen said. "It isn't a race." Her breath was jagged now. He was sure she was wanted to say more, but even she didn't have the breath to do so.

It is *a race*, David thought. *That's exactly what it is. If I get there and he's already risen . . .*

He let the thought fall away. If his dad had risen there was nothing he could do about it, and it wouldn't be his fault. *At least I tried to be here,* he thought. It felt like a lie. If there had been no one there to meet his father then it would be completely his fault—who else could take the blame?

But if his dad had already risen then the final chance to speak to him was lost.

The rucksack on his back weighed down on him. He bent forward until it felt like he was crawling up the steps, his fingertips brushing the ground. Sweat ran down the back of his neck to stick his T-shirt against his spine.

He blinked sweat out of his eyes and continued to step through the shadows. A tree overhung the path and low branches scratched at his shoulders like skeletal hands. He slipped the rucksack from his back and paused to take a moment's rest, peering down the hill to the car park. Another 4x4 entered the parking area, brilliant white headlamps splashed over the tarmac and the row of vehicles. From this distance the car's engine was a low hum, like an insect.

David turned to check the distance remaining to the top of the hill. "Why didn't mum get a plot near the bottom?" he asked. Helen didn't answer.

When the 4x4 turned off its headlamps the whole of the graveyard fell into darkness. Deeper than before. The small stone steps—uneven, and hard to find even when the light was on them, faded into invisibility.

"Let's give it a minute."

Shape gradually returned to the graveyard as his vision acclimatised to the gloom. He was more familiar with the burn of a city's lights on the horizon even in the dead of night, and the low hum of wheels on the tarmac of a motorway running twenty-four hours a day. The intensity of this darkness was strange.

In time he could pick out shapes huddled around headstones further down the hill. The only movement came from the latest arrival as they unloaded the back of the Jeep and gathered their equipment in a pile by the back wheel.

"How much stuff did he bring with him?" Helen asked.

"It doesn't matter," David said, his voice sharp. He couldn't see details, but he didn't need to know exactly what the Family Director carried for the vigil. The sheer quantity of equipment was enough to make him feel unprepared. "Let's go," he said roughly.

"You didn't tell me the tickets were in The Gods," Helen said behind him.

"What?"

"The Gods. You know . . . the top tier of a theatre."

He waved the beam from the torch over a row of headstones. "He's somewhere around here." He reached around to drop the rucksack onto the ground by Helen's feet. "Do you want to wait here while I go and check it out? There's no point the pair of us tracking up and down the rows lugging all this."

Helen made a sound.

"Are you okay?" David asked.

It was impossible to interpret the noise she made. He lifted the torch and she used her hands to stop the light from flooding her face. Her features were stark: black lines where the shadows began, the light picking out individual strands of her hair. She blinked rapidly. "Are you trying to blind me?"

"Sorry." He dropped the torch and the light cast a shadow behind Helen, like a wraith infecting the cemetery.

"Hurry up. The quicker we can sit down the better I'll feel."

"You're sure?" David asked again.

"Just go. If you're going to baby me the whole time we're here then there's no point in coming with you."

David refrained from saying he would have been perfectly okay doing this on his own. They were here now and there was no reason to drag up the arguments they'd had in the run-up to his dad's anniversary.

He turned his back on her and washed the torchlight down the aisle of gravestones on his left. The idea of stepping on the graves seemed disrespectful, but in the absence of a marked path, there was no alternative. And then he thought about the reason he was there and flashed the light over the closest grave. The dates were more than twenty years ago so it was safe.

The gravel from the first plot crunched under his boots as he placed his weight in the centre of the grave. He stepped onto the second plot—the surface covered in grass rather than stones this time. He slipped his feet along the edge of the plot as if that made any difference to the people underneath in their coffins.

Each time he passed from one grave to the next he checked the dates on the engraving, just to be certain. He was halfway down the row and turned back to discover Helen was only a dark outline pressed against the night.

This is madness, he thought. Helen was right—he should have paid the charge and left it to the professionals. It would have meant he didn't need to go crawling around in the darkness or lying to his mother about where he was going as if she wasn't able to add twenty years to the date of his father's death just as easily as he had done.

Too late now. He could either carry on and find his father's grave or walk back to the car and give up; leave his dad to the elements. He'd heard of people who did that—usually because they didn't have enough money to pay for a Family Director. As far as David was concerned, that wasn't an option. He wasn't going to abandon his father now.

Helen's outline waved him on, encouraging him to keep searching until he found the right name. He stumbled past Stephen West, Mark Bacon, Stuart May, and Peter Hughes. The graves were a mixture of ornate headstones with sweeping angels and carved arches alongside simple granite markers which carried only the name and relevant dates for those buried underneath. There was no one interred in the ground even within a year of the date David had etched onto his memory: 3rd March 2008. He'd only been five at the time and although he was sure he should remember everything about the day he suspected most of his memories were really piecemeal reconstructions of photographs and the rare snippets of information his mother let slip about her husband.

Sophie Miller had died in 2020. David quickly calculated in his head and realised he was reading the memorial of a young girl. There was a photograph behind a plastic disc fixed to the black marble. The image was water-logged and faded. In the centre of the grave was a steel flask containing fresh flowers. David wondered how often Sophie's parents travelled to the cemetery with the bunch of daisies and carnations wrapped in cellophane. Maybe it was just coincidence that he was there just after they had visited, but he didn't think so. Despite the blurred image of the girl, the grave gave the strong impression that it was tended with love.

He turned the beam away from the marble

headstone, conscious he was simply looking for an excuse not to move further along the line of graves.

The next grave was bare dirt. The gravel chips had been left in a pile at the foot of the grave like a duvet kicked off the bed on a hot night.

The dark soil had scratch marks where the sexton had dragged the blade of the shovel over the ground. There was a shallow recess in the middle of the plot as if the grave was beginning to collapse. It looked like an animal had tried to burrow its way down into the ground.

David turned the beam of the torch onto the headstone, even though he already knew what was written there.

Graham Chadwick
5 November 1971
3 March 2008

CHAPTER 3

"HELLO, DAD."

David spoke quietly, afraid his voice might carry to Helen. For weeks and months, he had planned what he was going to say but now when he heard his own words in the stillness of the graveyard it sounded false and insincere.

He looked down at the dirt and tried to imagine his father lying in a coffin deep underground. The brass plaque on the lid would be tarnished; the oak casket would be stained with water and dirt. David realised he was avoiding thinking about the inside of the coffin, whether the silk lining would have disintegrated, what his father's body looked like. He'd heard enough stories and seen enough photographs to prepare himself for the rising, but still, he found it impossible to reconcile those images with the truth of his dad lying down there in the dark.

Helen's hand curled around his arm, and he only just managed to stop himself from screaming. He hadn't noticed her creeping along the row of graves towards him. In the cold air she was the only source of warmth around. Her breath misted in front of the torch.

"Are you okay?" she asked. Her voice was gentle, and David decided maybe it wouldn't have been so terrible if she'd heard him speaking to his dad. Now that she was standing beside him, he was relieved Helen had insisted she accompany him.

He nodded in response to her question. It was probably not the whole truth, but he thought, in these circumstances, the definition of okay was flexible.

He noticed the bag was missing from Helen's back, and as soon as he realised that, he understood she'd left their pile of equipment at the end of the row, where the stone steps wound up into the hill. *All the better to sneak up on you*, he thought, and then laughed quietly. He was sure her decision to leave the equipment was practical; she'd wanted to be beside him, and the heavy bag had slowed her down.

"Better get set up, it's going to be a long night," he said.

"How long do you think . . . ?" Helen asked and then stopped herself from finishing the question.

"It will take as long as it takes."

Helen nodded as if this trite observation was the most profound comment she'd heard in many years. *It will take as long as it takes.*

God, I hope not, David thought.

"If nothing happens by the morning, you can head back into town and find a hotel room. There's no point both of us sitting out here freezing to death."

The shadows hid the worst of Helen's withering look, but David still caught enough to understand her disdain for his suggestion. He was relieved by her response; now that he was among the graves, he wasn't sure how well he would have fared on his own.

He glanced back along the headstones to the bags gathered on the steps and hesitated before handing Helen the torch. He glanced down at the ground. *It's too early . . . but still . . .*

"I'll get the bags."

"I can carry too. I'm not some feeble lady who needs the doors opening for her."

David smiled. "Don't I know that. It's just better if one of us waits here and holds the torch. Try and shine it on the ground in front of me so I don't turn an ankle unless you fancy carrying me down to the car park over your back."

She laughed. It was a thin sound, diminished by the cold and the wind. In the heavy atmosphere of the cemetery, it bordered on disrespectful without quite stepping over the line.

David walked back over the graves. The light behind him caused his shadow to stretch ahead like a thin monster. It dripped over the headstones, elongated fingers brushing across the marble surface.

He carried the bags in three trips, dumping them in a pile behind his father's headstone on the concrete capstone of Joseph Petersen. He felt the need to read the man's epitaph in apology for making such a racket six feet above his head. According to the engraving, Joseph had departed this world in 1976, so David wondered whether the concrete bed had been added since the turn of the century, or if Joseph was underneath, nails torn away from scratching on the underside of the concrete plug. The colour of the concrete and the multitude of lichen suggested maybe the concrete had been poured shortly after the grave was filled. *Some families are cruel bastards*, David thought.

"Whatever happens between us, when my time comes, don't just leave me under there to suffer," he said to Helen without really thinking of what he was saying. Only afterwards did he consider it suggested a longevity to their relationship which went beyond anything they had ever spoken about. Helen had her back to him. She didn't respond, and he couldn't decide if she simply hadn't heard him. Maybe he was reading too much into everything at the moment.

On the final trip he wrangled the large wooden chair up the hill. Cursing aloud each time the legs cracked against his shins. The weight dragged against the muscles of his arms until they felt like they had been stretched on a rack.

They unpacked the bags in silence. Set up the two camp chairs to look over the top of his father's gravestone. He put the torch into the cupholder of one of the chairs. Between the two chairs he placed the bag of food, a mixture of snacks to keep them going and more substantial meals if they were still there after dawn had broken. He left the pile of equipment at the side of the grave and when he looked at the leather straps and the metal fastenings he found himself praying he would never need to use most of it.

He sat down in the chair and heard the struts creak beside him as Helen did the same. He reached out and his hand met hers, a choreographed move repeated at cinemas and theatres, and other occasions where they found themselves sitting in darkness.

The light from the torch spilled across the black soil of his father's grave and illuminated the backs of the headstones for a few rows ahead. Beyond that, the darkness pressed against the light. Further away he could see the small pools of light where Family Directors had set up camp by some of the other graves. "Leeches," he muttered under his breath, but in the quiet of the graveyard, his whisper carried.

"They're just making a living," Helen replied.

He chose not to answer. They'd been a couple long enough for him to realise when he was steering towards an argument. Nothing Helen could say would persuade him that the men in their charcoal grey suits and black ties served any purpose except to rip off scared and grieving families. He'd put his own details into their websites to get a quote for their services— mostly just to get a better idea of what he needed to do to prepare himself, but also out of curiosity. The fees they charged were obscene, but worse than that were the scare tactics they used—photographs blurred out of a faux sense of decency. They showed the risen— desiccated flesh wrapped tight around stick bones. Faces stretched back to rictus grins where the cartilage in the nose had rotted away to leave a black space. They showed nails as long as talons, eye sockets where spiders lived. They were a horror show, no other way to describe it. A horror show designed to frighten families into handing over a wad of cash and saying, *I don't want to see my loved one like that, you deal with it.*

"I went to see one with my mother," he said. He held his voice low so his words did not carry along the valley to the men down there.

"When?"

"Last year, when we started to talk about the twenty-year anniversary. Up until then, we both chose to pretend it was never going to happen. You have to get in early; these outfits book up fast and it isn't like you can change the date if there's no one available. It's why they get away with charging obscene amounts—they feed off the fear that if you can't use a *respectable* outfit like them,"—David leaned hard on the word respectable just so there could be no doubt he didn't share the assessment—"then you're left flailing around the backstreets to hire a couple of guys with a spade and a rusted old iron chain. Who wants that for their loved ones?"

He could sense Helen trying to decide whether to reply.

"You do it yourself. For your family," he said. "It's the right way."

"I don't know . . . "

"It's okay for you; both of your parents are still alive."

Helen's hand slipped out of his. He felt her withdrawing—not just physically but emotionally. "I'm sorry," he said, but the apology sounded insincere. He left his hand dangling in the no-man's land between them.

"I saw a boy die," Helen said. "He was in my class at primary school. He stepped onto the road and a car hit him. He was knocked into a wall and sat there with one shoulder lower than the other as if he had been propped there for someone to find."

"It's not the same . . . "

"No, it isn't." Helen's voice rose to a shout. "He was just a kid and he was dead, and a few years from now his parents are going to have to make a decision on how to deal with his twentieth anniversary. Do you think they should have to sit out on this hill and wait for him to rise? Do you think they should arm themselves with chains and restraints and all of the shit you've got there? When their kid wakes up and starts clawing through the air should they be the ones to deal with it?"

"It's different . . . " David started to say, and then fell silent. It was an argument he didn't need to win. Whatever happened to the kid in Helen's class was a tragedy and he didn't know how any parent could watch their child rise, but that wasn't what he was saying.

The gap between them was only a couple of inches but at the moment it felt like a gulf of miles. David heard her weeping. He reached out a hand to touch her arm and she shrugged it away in a violent motion.

"I'm sorry," he said again, and this time his words carried some emotional weight, but too little to make an impact.

He checked his watch, waving his arm in front of the torch beam. It was nearly seven. Later than he'd intended to be set up, but it was still at least five hours before anything could happen. He watched the small huddles around the hill and wondered who would rise first.

CHAPTER 4

THEIR RECORD WAS three weeks without speaking. David sat huddled inside his jacket, cursing himself for not bringing more layers of clothing, and tried to remember what they had been arguing about on that occasion. He could have asked Helen but dismissed the idea the moment it entered his head. He listened to her shallow breathing and the creak of her chair as she moved. There was nothing to suggest a thaw in her mood and he reminded himself she had only been silent for an hour. Helen Yates was not even starting.

He ran through half a dozen different ways to apologise but none of them made it past his lips. Mostly he was silent because he genuinely couldn't decide on the right thing to say, but he was honest enough to accept there was a degree of stubbornness in his own silence. *Stubborn as a mule*, his mum would often tell him when he was younger, and once when he and Helen had both sat in simmering silence in the back of her car during a drive down to London she'd told the pair they were stubborn enough to start a war by accident.

He wanted to point out to Helen that they were

holding vigil over his father's grave; if anyone had the right to be emotional, then it was him. She was supposed to be there to support him. He tried the argument in his mind and abandoned it. Three weeks was a long time to remain locked in war.

He dragged over one of the rucksacks and rummaged through the side pockets until he found some chocolate. He unwrapped two bars and handed the Snickers across to Helen. It hung in the air, an unaccepted gift. He wanted to believe she was either asleep or just didn't notice the peace offering. "Do you want . . . ?" he started. Helen turned toward him. The darkness hid most of her features, so he was spared the withering look he was confident waited for him. "Suit yourself," he muttered. He tucked the chocolate bar into the pocket of Helen's chair. She could eat or go hungry; it didn't make any difference to him. Three hours, three days, three weeks. She was a grown-up, she could make her own decisions.

"Hey, Kid!"

The voice came out of the dark. David turned in the direction of the sound but saw nothing except shadows. He peered through the gloom. Behind him, Helen's chair creaked and a moment later her torch shifted focus from his father's grave to the wide swath of cemetery in front of them.

The man put his hand up to his face to shield himself from the glare of the torch. He looked like a convict trapped by a searchlight. He was over six foot and thin as a stick. He wore a black two-piece suit that immediately marked him out as a Family Director. David's lip automatically curled up in disgust. The suit looked cheap and a poor fit, baggy around the waist as if it were intended for a larger man.

"You trying to blind me?" he asked.

"Well don't go sneaking up on people," Helen said.

"I wasn't. I called out to yous, dint I?" There was a whining tone to his voice that immediately set David against him as if David needed any other reason to loathe the man.

The Family Director took a couple of steps closer, still holding his hands in front of him. The top button of his shirt was undone. His tie was loosened and pulled askew as if he were coming home from a long day at the office. He stepped over the concrete border of a grave to stand in the middle of Sophie Miller's plot. He raised a foot to step onto the soil of Graham Chadwick's grave.

"Don't."

David's single command stopped the man's foot in mid-air before he retraced his step to stand in the next-door grave.

"What are you kids doing here?"

"Fishing," Helen said before David could come up with a suitable response. "We've heard the sport here is great."

"Huck-huck." The man's laughter was false and forced. "Yous don't want to be out here on your own. Two young kids." He glanced down at the ground around his shoes and delicately stepped onto the concrete grave surround and tightrope-walked his way around the edge of Graham Chadwick's grave until he stood by Helen's side.

She lifted the torch to pin him squarely within its beam. Close up, the flushed complexion of his face was evident. Beads of sweat stippled his forehead. He had long, wiry hair; black, fading to grey at the roots. When he ran his hand through his hair the strands stood up like spiked grass.

"What I mean to be saying is that kids your age don't need to be out here. This isn't something you should be dealing with. That's what the professionals are for."

So that's your pitch? David thought. Someone had latched onto what was possibly the only thing more grotesque than running a business and pushing images of the rising at grieving families: waiting for the families to set up at the graveside and trying to win their business then.

The Family Director leaned forward. "Have you ever seen a rising? I mean in real-life, not just on a pitcher screen? It isn't like the movies where the person comes out and it looks like they've put on new clothes 'specially for the occasion and they're all clean and neat. It's horrible. I say that myself and I have to deal with it every day and I suppose I've become immune to it. But it's still horrible."

"Fuck off," David said.

The thin man continued speaking. "I was looking after a woman just last week and when she came up, she had fat white maggots hanging out of her skin. She'd been in an accident and most of her face was missing so even her own fambly wouldn't have recognised her. That isn't the last memory you want of . . . "

He paused to read the writing on the gravestone. David could sense the man working through the dates etched into the marble. "Your dad . . . " He spoke with hesitancy, testing his assumption. "You want to remember your dad as he was, not the corpse lying under the ground. I promise you that memory will

24

haunt you for the rest of your life. I saw a fambly here just last week and they insisted on staying for the rising. It was a beloved grandfather and they must have thought they'd get one last chance to spend some time with him and instead what they got was a horror show where—"

"Fuck off," David said again. Louder.

The thin man glanced at him, dismissed him, and returned his attention to Helen. "I don't want you to experience that. When it was my mother's time to rise, I arranged for a friend in the business to look after her. That way I knew she was cared for during her last few minutes."

"That's very thoughtful."

The thin man took Helen's comment as encouragement to continue his marketing spiel. David could have warned him, but he sat back to watch what would happen next. He'd been on the receiving end of Helen's criticism often enough to appreciate when it was aimed at someone else.

"I'm just here to offer a service to people when they're down."

"You mean you're here to prey on people when they're vulnerable?"

"No." Even in the gloom, David could see the change in the man's features as he realised Helen wasn't going to be the easy sell he'd assumed. He hesitated before making a proper reply. "People *are* vulnerable, you're right. And when people are emotional, they don't always make the right decisions."

"You're saying I'm too emotional to think straight?"

"That's not what I meant."

David watched the man squirm. To give him his credit, he didn't look like giving up. Maybe spending each day trawling the graveyard for business inured him against all but the worst criticisms people levelled at him.

"It's the media's fault. There's all these films and documentaries and books about the rising which suggest it's an opportunity to make amends. It isn't anything like that. I've helped hundreds of people through the rising. I can tell you now that whatever you're looking for by coming here, you're not going to get."

"Thanks for the advice."

"I can take that pain away from you. I didn't know your father, but I don't believe he would have wanted you to sit through this."

David waited for Helen to correct him, but she let the thin man carry on with his mistake.

"There's still time. I've got professional equipment in the van." He looked down at the soil. "No sign of movement yet, so I figure I can get set up and you can be gone. You can leave me your details and I'll give you a full report afterwards, written up and everything."

"How much?" David asked.

His price was less than half David had been quoted by any of the reputable companies his mother had contacted. What did that mean? Would the thin man even bother to stay around after they had handed over the money? Perhaps he would wait until they had driven out of the car park and then leave minutes later so Graham Chadwick could go through the rising on his own.

David spotted the movement just a moment before he noticed a second man approaching them. *Here comes the cavalry*, he thought. Now the thin man had them hooked here was his associate to seal the deal. The latest arrival was also dressed in a dark suit – but better quality material than the thin man's clothes. He was almost a foot shorter and carried himself with the stocky movement of someone who spent time lifting weights.

"Get lost, Nathaniel."

Nathaniel turned to the newcomer. "Haven't you got a job to look after?"

"Yes, I have, which is why I'm not up on the hill pestering poor folks who've just come along to care for their own dead. It's people like you who give the business a bad name."

"People like me?" Nathaniel turned to confront the newcomer, planting a dirty shoe in the middle of Graham Chadwick's grave.

They're going to start a brawl over my dad's grave. David rose from the chair to move closer. He could smell the stink coming off Nathaniel—a mix of cheap alcohol and sweat. The newcomer glanced at him, a fleeting look that managed to suggest everything would be okay and he didn't need to get involved. Still, David stood there, not sure what he was supposed to do but damned if he was going to have a pair of grown men fighting above his dad. What if his father started to rise while they were still there? What would he think then?

"Go home, Nathaniel," the newcomer said. His words were tired; a fatigued air which suggested he was too bored to fight him. "Find a proper job, something you're actually good at."

"Don't you tell me what to do. Who do you think you are?"

The newcomer didn't answer. This close, David saw the muscles in his arms and neck more clearly. He seemed to have been poured into his funeral suit. He was the sort of man David would have made a point of avoiding if he came across him late at night. In the pale torchlight, David glimpsed a black tattoo rising up from beneath the button-downed neck of a white shirt. The ink stretched across his throat and stopped just under his chin.

"I was here first," Nathaniel said. He sounded like a petulant child.

David stared down at the foot still solidly placed in the middle of his father's grave. That thoughtless sacrilege affected him more than the pathetic attempt of the man to drum up some business with his horror stories.

"I want you to go. Now," David said.

Nathaniel at least had the decency to look like he was considering the request, even if he did not reply. Or move his foot.

David wondered what it was actually going to take to get the leech to leave them alone. In the usual course of things—if Nathaniel were a beggar on the High Street—David would simply have walked away, but that wasn't an option here.

"Look, you're wasting your time. I'm not going to pay you. If I wanted a Family Director I would have sorted it years ago, not waited until I got here to see what I can find. You can stand on my dad's grave until he rises—I'm not going to stop you—but just know you're not going to see a penny from me."

Finally, Nathaniel stepped onto the concrete surround. He almost looked embarrassed, but David

thought it was probably more likely he'd just realised the impact of his mistake. Still, he didn't give up. "I can help you. I know you don't think you need any assistance, but I don't want you to have to go through this alone."

"You're all heart," Helen said from her seat at the back of the grave. "We've heard your pitch, now please leave."

"I've seen your type before." He gestured to the equipment David had laid out. "You think you know what you're doing. You've bought the tools and watched the YouTube videos. You bought yourself a heavy wooden chair because that's what all the websites tell you to get, but you don't even know why it has to be wood. You think you can do it alone, but I'm telling you that isn't the case." He almost sounded genuine. Almost. David was sure he was watching a performance the thin man had perfected over years. Maybe he knew from experience that if he refused to leave, they would end up giving him money just to get rid of him. David had about £50 in cash in his wallet. He wondered if that would be enough, or whether the guy would take out a chip & pin reader and offer to accept payment by credit card.

From the folds of darkness, the squat man drifted back into the scene, ignoring Helen and David and focussed only on the other Funeral Director. "Leave, Nathaniel. They're not desperate enough or stupid enough to need you."

Nathaniel opened his mouth to make one last attempt to win them over but closed his lips without speaking. He stalked off into the darkness of the cemetery, his footsteps fading as his shape dissolved into the night.

The newcomer stood, half-hidden in shadows. Waiting to be invited forwards, David thought. *So that's the game—good cop, bad cop. Nathaniel comes to soften us up and then his partner arrives to chuck him out.* He wondered whether they alternated the roles each time they played out the charade, but he found it difficult to imagine Nathaniel as the respectable half of the duo.

"I meant what I said. I don't need help."

The man took a step forward so he was fully inside the beam of the torch. He stepped onto the concrete surround, glanced at the headstone at the top of the grave, and then blessed himself quickly—pressing his fingertips against his head, chest and shoulders. He muttered something inaudible.

David bristled. *Don't you go praying for my dad.* Before he said anything, he sensed Helen stand up from her chair to take a place beside him.

"You're wrong," the man said. "Managing a rising isn't something for an amateur. It doesn't matter how many websites you've visited and how much equipment you've brought with you. And as much as Nathaniel is a prick that I wouldn't trust to look after a children's party, he's absolutely right—you should never try and manage the rising of one of your own."

"Let me guess, it just so happens you can offer me a good rate?"

The man winced and waved his hands. "No. I'm responsible for another gentleman further down the hill. I couldn't take on your father's rising even if you begged. I can give you some contacts in case you change your mind. Professionals, not like Nathaniel.

People I trust. Most of them will probably not be available but I'm happy to help you find someone."

"No thanks."

The man reached forward and held out his hand. "Billy," he said as he shook with David and then with Helen. He nodded down at the headstone. "I'm sorry for your loss."

"Thanks. It was a long time ago."

"It always is." Billy peered at him and David felt himself being inspected. "You couldn't have been old when your father passed on."

"I was just five."

Billy shook his head in sympathy. To David the emotion seemed genuine, but he was too aware of how easy he could be manipulated at the moment.

"When is he due?" Billy asked.

"Tomorrow."

"I can read the date. I mean *when* is he due?"

David wondered if it was a trick question to make him feel stupid, if so, it worked. He didn't even understand what he was being asked.

The confusion must have shown on his face as Billy explained the question. "What time did your father die?"

"I don't know."

"Is there no one you could ask? A sibling? Your mother?"

"I don't have any brothers or sisters, and my mum doesn't talk about dad. She thinks I hired one of you lot to deal with this."

If Billy noticed the insult buried in the response, he chose to ignore it. He tapped his fingernails against his teeth as he thought. "It's not a problem. Happens a lot; more than you'd expect. Pass me your stethoscope."

"What?"

Billy walked over to where the rucksacks were piled high behind the headstone. "I only came to stop Nathaniel, but if you hand me your stethoscope, I can do a quick check and give you an idea how long you're going to be waiting. It helps you prepare yourself."

"I don't have a stethoscope."

"Why not? It's on the lists. Even if you check the most inept website, it's always on the list of essential equipment to buy."

David shrugged. He could feel his neck getting hot with embarrassment. "I didn't think I'd need one. It just seemed . . . " his excuse tailed off.

"Were you planning to hold a glass against the ground to hear when your father started rising?" A look of frustration crossed Billy's face and although he said nothing, David knew exactly what the Family Director was thinking: *Amateurs.*

"Have you got *anything* I can use?"

"No," David said quietly. He was aware of Helen standing beside his shoulder and although she hadn't said a word, he knew she was desperate to point out that this just proved she was right—he needed someone professional.

"I'm fine. I can manage," David said. "You can go back to your own plot. Leave me to deal with my dad."

Billy stood staring at him for a moment and David assumed he was going to end up in a similar fight to the one that had just finished with Nathaniel. "Why can't you lot just leave me alone?"

There was another moment of silence and then Billy nodded. "You're right. Of course, you're right. None of my business."

He turned away. For a second David thought the man would touch the brim of a non-existent Stetson in farewell, but instead he simply picked his way across the graves, balancing on one concrete surround and then the next until he had melted back into the darkness.

CHAPTER 5

DAVID SPENT TWENTY minutes on his haunches in the near dark sorting through the rucksacks and laying out his equipment on the ragged grass of an old grave, just so he didn't have to sit in silence beside Helen and wait for her to point out what an idiot he was. How was he supposed to know a stethoscope was important? Even a second hand one would have cost a small fortune and when he had been totting up everything he needed to buy for the rising it had just seemed extravagant. He wanted to ask Helen: What was I supposed to leave out to pay for the stethoscope? The spade? The restraints? But he knew what her response would be, because it was as inevitable as the rising: *For the amount of money you spent on all the equipment, you could have hired a Family Director.* Just because she was right, that didn't make it any easier to have the conversation.

He took the sheet of paper from the pocket of a rucksack and used his torch to light up the script, even though he had each word committed to memory. Still, he read the speech to calm his thoughts.

Graham Chadwick. I am David Chadwick and I am your son.

When the roar of fear had settled to a dull ache, he returned the tattered page to the bag and continued sorting through the rest of the gear.

Despite the cool of the night, he was hot from shifting all the equipment. He wiped sweat from his face with a handkerchief and sank back into the chair and waited for his breathing to return to normal. From the other side of the graveyard, he heard a shout, but the distance was so great, the words were muffled and it felt unreal.

"Do you think Billy has got his Rising?" he asked Helen.

He thought she might not answer, that she was harbouring grudge laid upon grudge and her three-week record might be challenged. They were supposed to be going to London in a month, he hoped the chill would have thawed before then or it could be an uncomfortable weekend.

"It sounds too far away. I figure he must have come from one of the rows a little further down the hill. Maybe that one over there."

David peered at one of the small balls of light in the distance. The quality of the light suggested the torch being used was muted. It made it difficult to accurately judge the distance, but it looked too close to be the source of the voices he heard.

"What if he doesn't say anything?" Helen asked.

"I've read enough to be realistic—he might not be able to talk, or he might not be in the right state to listen to anything I have to say, but it's the only chance I'm ever going to get. Mum is never going to answer my questions. You've been at her house . . . "

"Great roast potatoes, but I know what you mean.

From the look of your mum's house, your father never existed. All the photos around the mantelpieces are of her or you."

"Maybe they didn't have cameras back then," David joked.

"But she was able to take hundreds of you from before the age of five. Do you know why she's like that?"

"If I ever mention dad, she changes the subject." He was silent for a moment, thinking about all the frustration he felt over the years.

"I only have his photograph by accident. If it were up to mum, I wouldn't even know what he looked like. It's like she can't forgive him for dying. As if he had a choice.

"Mum refuses to mention him. She'd prefer to believe I was the result of an immaculate conception. When I was a kid, I used to think she was too sad to talk about him, but as I got older, I realised her emotion was anger rather than sadness."

"Maybe she's angry because he left her. I know it wasn't his fault he died, but people aren't always rational."

"Maybe," David said, but he could tell Helen knew he didn't agree with the diagnosis. "When I was about eighteen we had a blazing row about him. Screaming, plates smashing, the whole works. I said she had no right to take him away from me. He was my father and she couldn't just erase him from my life."

"I assume that worked?"

Billy laughed. "No. Not really." This was the part he couldn't explain, not to his mother, not to Helen. Not to anyone. They just didn't get it. If they did they would never have tried to stop him from coming to the rising because they would have known he had to be there. There was a piece of him missing. A book with pages stuck together and he just had to know what was written on them. His dad was a part of him; nature/nurture—all that crap.

Helen was silent, but there was nothing prickly about the lack of conversation this time. Clearly, he'd been forgiven.

He tried to focus on the lights on the far side of the cemetery. Inside one of those balls of pale illumination, a Family Director was trying to handle one of the risen. What was it *really* like? He'd watched videos on YouTube. He'd seen the History Live! series that followed a Family Director over the course of a year, but even then the camera shied away during the rising; the filmmakers coy about the details, as if they were filming a murder or a couple having sex.

There was a loud yelp. David jumped to his feet. One of the lights flickered and grew brighter. It was too far away for him to see any details; Helen was right—it was on the far side of the cemetery. He wondered if Nathaniel might have shuffled over that way to offer a hand. For a price.

"When it happens, you need to stay away. You promised," he reminded Helen.

"I know."

"At that point you could start to make your way down to the car. Just in case you need to get help."

"If you need any help it would be too late by the time I come back with anyone. It's a twenty-minute drive to the nearest town. Assuming I could even find someone willing to come to the cemetery with me."

"Maybe we should have accepted Nathaniel's offer of help after all," David said.

"Maybe," Helen said, in a tone that suggested he should have stopped being so stubborn and got the professionals in long ago. She still didn't get it. Maybe she never would. Probably. Both her parents were still alive.

"I found my parents' wedding album. It was under a pile of blankets in mum's wardrobe. She was livid. Asked me what I was doing snooping around her room. Didn't I understand the concept of privacy?"

"She had a point."

"I was only eight years old. John Gill had told me there was no such thing as Santa Claus—that it was just your parents and if you looked hard enough you could find your Christmas presents. So I did."

He reached out his hand to her. In the darkness Helen took it without hesitation. Her palm was soft. Warm.

"Most of the album was empty. I think she'd burned all of the photographs of my father."

There was a long pause before Helen said anything as if she was trying to decide how to respond. "Why?"

"I think she kept the wedding album because . . . well I don't know for sure and she never told me. She just took it away from me and the next time I went to look in her wardrobe it wasn't there. I was never able to find out where she hid it after that. I don't think she burned it. It was too precious for her—it had pictures of her friends and a few members of her family who are dead now."

He'd tried to imagine what his father had done to deserve being erased from history. It was just another question his mother refused to answer.

"I'm sorry," Helen said." She squeezed his hand.

From the other side of the cemetery came a howl, like an animal caught in a trap. David felt his whole body stiffen in response to the sound.

"I don't think I'm ready for this," he confessed. "You were right. I should have got someone professional to stay with me."

"Do you want me to go and find Nathaniel, I'm sure he's still loitering around here somewhere?"

David laughed quietly, afraid whatever was screaming at the other side of the cemetery might hear him and head in his direction. "Someone professional, I said."

He thought about the equipment laid out on the grass behind him. He'd had to remove most of the stuff from its packaging. New. Alien.

"Besides," he told her, "It's too late now. He'll be here soon."

CHAPTER 6

THE SCREAMING STOPPED after about thirty minutes. Longer than David had expected but not as long as he'd heard some risings take. He'd read about one Family Director who had supported a rising for three hours. Three hours with that screaming going on? The idea filled David's stomach with a low, churning dread.

After the screaming came the silence. And the darkness. The light at the other side of the cemetery blinked out and it felt like the night had rushed in to reclaim the plot. David imagined the Family Director sitting next to the open grave. Sweat soaked through his crumpled white shirt until it stained the silk lining of his black suit. It was a tough job—physical and emotional. Maybe that was why they charged so much. Maybe they did earn their pay after all.

"You should go."

Helen snorted her derision at the suggestion. She had every right to leave—she'd spent most of the last month begging, pleading, and eventually shouting at him to see sense and get someone in to do it properly. It wasn't safe for her there, but when she made it clear she was staying, the sense of relief flooded through his bones.

"And leave you alone to deal with this? You'd never forgive me . . . "

"Yes, I would."

" . . . and I'd never forgive myself," Helen said.

He realised they were both whispering. Their words barely loud enough to bridge the short distance between the two chairs. When he fell silent the quiet of the cemetery was oppressive as if it had weight. He struggled to breathe—it was his own sense of panic, he understood that—but still he felt the bands of his ribs tighten around his lungs. He gripped Helen's hand and tried to focus on his breathing, just as the therapist had taught him. In through the nose. Out through the mouth. In through the nose. Out through the mouth. Counting to ten each time before starting again. Helen didn't interrupt him until his breathing had returned to something close to normal.

"You okay?"

He nodded, and then realised she wouldn't be able to see the movement unless she was looking directly at him. "Yes," he managed to say. The word came out too high, like steam from a boiling kettle, but he thought it was probably the truth. His chest didn't feel as tight anymore. He didn't feel he had to focus all his attention on remembering to breathe.

"What if we both left?"

Helen asked the question so softly David wasn't even sure he'd heard her correctly. The words burned with a quiet shame.

"It happens," Helen said. "Not every rising is managed."

David was appalled to find himself considering the suggestion; just pack up everything and head back down to the car. Go and never come back. In fact, they didn't even need to pack up, they could run down the hill now and leave all the equipment piled up. Nathaniel or one of the other Family Directors would find the cache in the morning and they would surely put it to good use.

"I can't," David said, worried Helen would have noted how long it had taken him to reply. From now on, he would always be the son who had actually considered leaving his father to rise unattended. Even if he had only countenanced the suggestion for a few seconds.

Her hand squeezed his as if she were holding on to him.

The silence of the cemetery washed over David. *What have I done?* he asked himself, but the questions were too difficult to face. Instead, he peered down at the surface of his father's grave. There was no sign of movement.

A figure drifted into the liminal area of the torch's beam. A vague outline and David jerked with shock as the shape seemed to lunge toward the grave.

For a long second David could not react. The world stopped turning on its axis. Time halted.

One of the dead had completed their rising unattended and had been drawn towards the light.

David opened his mouth, trapped between shouting and screaming. The creature moved carefully over the ground, picking out each step. Something about the outline suggested to David that it was male. Had been male. Once. When it had been anything at all.

Involuntarily he sucked in a lungful of air and dropped Helen's hand. He heard a similar gasp from her but didn't dare turn away from the oncoming creature. He could feel his heart fluttering and he wondered whether it was possible to die of fright. To drop stone dead from fear at seeing one of the creatures up close.

It can't harm me, David thought. It was probably true, but he didn't find solace in the idea. The risen was a creature from a horror movie.

As the man stumbled into the light the pale glow washed over Billy's features. David breathed out. "Fuck. You scared the shit out of me."

"Sorry. I didn't think," the Director said. He held up his hand. It looked like he was grasping a snake and it took a moment for David to identify the stethoscope. "I know you said you didn't need any help. You were very clear on that and I respect your wishes, but I thought it couldn't hurt to have a quick check. There's no heroism to be had in flying blind when you've never even been inside a plane before."

The tubing of the stethoscope was red. The metal disc at the end had presumably been silver when it had first been made but it was now caked in mud and dirt.

Billy held out the stethoscope in front of him. David wasn't sure if the Director was offering to take a sounding himself or if he was providing the equipment for David to use. That David didn't know what he was supposed to be listening for or how to interpret any sound he might hear was a secondary issue.

"That's very thoughtful of you," Helen said. "How accurate is it?"

"As with any equipment, it all depends on the skill of the person using it. I can probably give you a one hour window for when Graham is going to rise."

He looked at David. "Do you want me to listen?"

One hour. To know when his father was going to rise was a gift David didn't even believe was possible. It offered him the chance to be properly prepared. To know if he was still going to be sitting there in fifteen hours' time, barely awake, nerves torn to shreds from every noise across the cemetery. Watching the ground to spot the first tremble as his father started rising.

"Please."

Billy took a moment to survey the length of the grave before kneeling on the ground. There was a delicate reverence to his movement that made David think of a priest at an altar. The Director fitted the ends of the stethoscope into his ears and gently placed a hand flat on the ground as if testing the temperature. He turned his head to one side, listening intently as he pushed the diaphragm into the dirt.

"How do you –"

Billy held his hand up and David stopped speaking. The Director withdrew the end of the stethoscope from the soil, looked around for a few seconds, and then buried it again. After a long wait, he looked up and shook his head. "Are you sure the date's correct?"

"Of course." David stopped and thought about that for a moment. "At least, it's the only information I have to go on."

"You don't have anything that would be able to confirm when he died? A death certificate? An article from the media?"

"The third of March. I've always known my father died on the third of March. It's about the only thing I do know about him."

Billy shrugged. "It's possible he's just very quiet. It

happens. That's not to say that he won't get louder as it gets closer to his time. The only thing I can tell you is that you've got at least a twelve hours wait ahead of you."

"Thank you," Helen said quickly.

"Yes. Thanks," David said. It was difficult to acknowledge that the Director had been helpful. He wanted to believe the man was still trying to trick him. But he couldn't see how the man benefitted from saying his father wouldn't rise for at least the next twelve hours.

"Which means you don't have to stand guard over here. You can go down and catch a few hours rest in your car. You're going to need to be alert when your dad is rising so it's best not to try and stay awake the whole night."

Do you honestly think I'm going to be able to sleep? David wondered. He thought about the cramped conditions in the cab of the truck. He and Helen would have to sleep sitting upright unless they lay under the stars on the flatbed behind the cab.

"Before you do, though. My client will be rising in about half an hour. It might help prepare you if you want to come down and watch what happens. No two risings are the same, but at least you'll have some idea of what you're going to face."

"Let me guess. That means you'd be free to help out with my father's rising also. At a price."

David sensed, rather than heard, Helen's disgust at his accusation. But the guy was a con artist, no different to Nathaniel, just a little more convincing.

"Sorry, you're on your own. Once I'm done here I'm heading home for a rest. I've got another booking for tomorrow night, so I need my beauty sleep. I'm just trying to be neighbourly."

David stared at the man kneeling on the ground above his father's coffin. The cuffs of his jacket were covered in mud. The knees of his trousers were stained dark brown. The yellow light from the torch washed over his face, casting shadows across his features.

Do I trust him?

No. That was the simple answer. He was a Family Director; the safest approach was to assume he was there for the money. If he was right then he'd saved himself from a world of hurt, as well as a chunk of money that would miraculously have transferred itself out of his pocket. And if he was wrong he had offended a man he would never see again. A man who must already have heard much worse said about him.

Do I need *to trust him?*

It *would* be useful to watch a Family Director conducting a rising. David had read the advice, watched the videos, bought the equipment. He felt prepared. As prepared as anyone could be. But . . . there was still that misgiving that he'd never actually seen a rising.

Billy waited patiently for the answer.

"Okay." David heard his mother's voice in his head, *What do you say?* "Thanks," he added. "I appreciate this."

"Nothing to thank me for. As long as you stay out of the way when the time comes it makes no difference to me."

Billy stood up and brushed at his knees, but the act did nothing to remove the patch of brown mud clinging to his trousers. He took the stethoscope out of his ears and hung it around his neck like a child playing at being a doctor.

"If you want, I'll check on him before I leave for the day," he offered. "By then we might have a better idea of when he's planning to rise."

"Thanks," David said again. It rankled that he found himself constantly expressing his gratitude to the man.

"Bring your spade with you. You might as well make yourself useful." The words sounded vaguely like a threat. David told himself he was just being overly sensitive; it was just a request.

Helen picked the torch up from the ground. For a moment the beam splashed into the sky and the area around them was black. In the darkness, David thought he heard the sound of nails scratching against wood.

"Lead on, MacDuff," Helen said. She pointed the torch down to the ground where the light spread out between the graves like marsh gas. Once they started moving, David could only hear the sound of blood rushing through his own head and the crunch of their footsteps as they stepped between the graves.

Billy led them down the hill, finding paths where there were none, weaving between the headstones, never stepping on a grave. Down they went until they stopped beside the headstone of Reginald Wooley.

CHAPTER 7

THERE WERE TWO chairs by the grave. A solid wooden chair similar to the one David had lugged up the hillside himself, and a small canvas seat. A backpack was open on the ground with a collection of small bags inside. A Tupperware box which David assumed contained the Director's lunch, and a bottle of Sainsbury's Valu brand still water.

David realised that since entering the cemetery he had formed a habit of reading all the headstones he passed and doing a quick mental calculation to determine when the occupants reached their twenty-year anniversary. Reginald Wooley died a day before Graham Chadwick: 2nd March 2008. *Not long to go then*, David thought. *Just a few hours until the day is over*. Almost all of the other graves in the cemetery were older; twenty-five, thirty, thirty-five. The neighbouring grave had the telltale mark of a rising where the earth had then fallen down into the coffin. On the other side of Reginald was a plot for Rosie MacBride. She'd been in the ground for less than a year. The earth still looked scarred from her interring.

David cast a glance at the equipment laid out behind Reginald Wooley's grave. He didn't want to give Billy the satisfaction of knowing his preparation was being inspected, so he took a sly half-look but he was relieved to see the display was similar to his own; both in terms of layout and tools. The restraints were closest; the most likely to be used and therefore first to be reached. At the far end of the row of tools were the spade and the steel chain. David shuddered at the last, hoping it would never be needed.

The equipment looked old, but well maintained. He wanted to take a closer look, but instead he cast a glance around before settling on the raised stone sarcophagus of the grave of Marcus and Angela Quigley. The cold of the stone seeped through the denim of his jeans in seconds. It prompted him to think of his father lying in his coffin; surrounded by a thin layer of silk and padding. He wondered if the insulation had any real success at keeping out the cold and the damp.

Billy knelt down next to the headstone and placed the stethoscope back in his ears. He pressed the bell of the device deep into the soil and then took soundings from a few different positions across the grave before standing up.

"Sorry, I didn't bring spare chairs," Billy said. "Except . . . " he motioned to the wooden chair beside his own. David looked at it and shivered.

"No thanks. I'm fine where I am."

Billy laughed. Low. Quiet. Not entirely pleasant.

"Are you really superstitious? There's no harm in taking the Dead Man's Seat. It's not like he's going to complain when he starts rising. Helen?"

David felt her shiver against him at the prospect of sitting in the chair. She snaked a hand through his arm and pressed tightly to him. The chair itself was an innocuous thing; more sturdy than the foldaway camp seat which Billy occupied. It had wooden sides and a wooden back. *All the better to tie you to*, David thought to himself.

"Some don't use the chair anyway," Billy said. "After being trapped in a box underground most of them choose to walk. It's like watching a fish circling inside a bowl."

"Do they ever try and run for it?" Helen asked.

"Occasionally," Billy said, as if it was the most natural question in the world.

David thought about having to chase one of the newly risen across the graves. "Presumably they don't get too far?"

"You'd be surprised. They've had twenty years down there to plot and plan. Can you imagine that? Twenty years lying in the darkness waiting for the moment you know is coming. Your only chance. Even if you accept it's not going to last very long there are still some people who think they can outrun the inevitable. I had a friend . . . well, more of a colleague . . . he was overseeing a rising down in Broadstairs when the client came out of the grave at a run and nearly made it into the town centre before Alan caught up with him and managed to shackle him." Billy grinned as he spoke.

"That ever happen to you?"

Billy waved his hand to take in the chair and the equipment laid out on the tarpaulin mat. "Do I look like the sort of amateur who would let a rising get away from me? I've been doing this for thirty years now."

"You don't look old enough," Helen said.

Billy tipped a non-existent hat at the observation. "Well thank you, Ma'am. I'll take that as a compliment. I started as an apprentice with the Co-op. Worked for them for nearly ten years until I was able to save enough to buy my gear and set up on my own."

"Why?" David asked.

"More freedom. When I was with the Co-op . . . "

"I mean why this job?"

Billy looked like he didn't really understand the question. He sat back in his chair, peering up at the sky. "It's a good job. You get to meet lots of people. You get to *help* lots of people."

"But if you just wanted to help people you could have done the same working in a hospital or a library."

"It's a respected profession."

"I'm sorry, I'm sure David wasn't trying to imply anything with his question," Helen said. She glared at him, suggesting that all three of them knew full well that he absolutely was trying to imply that no sane, normal person would take up a job as a Family Director. "It's just that it doesn't seem the sort of career choice a nineteen-year-old boy would make."

"My father was a Family Director, and his father before that. The career goes back at least four generations, maybe more. I go home at night and sleep knowing I made a difference to one family." He looked up at Helen. "Can you honestly say that?"

She shrugged. "I'm an accountant. So no, probably not. I spend all day in an office with a window that looks out on a car park, but I don't notice the lack of a view because I'm just staring at the screen trying to work through a list of numbers. I tell myself it's a public service —you've probably got some of your pension invested in these companies and it's my job to make sure they're telling the truth about their money—but most days it's just a job."

David had never heard her talk about her career that way before. The suggestion that it might have a higher value than something which paid the bills and her contribution to their holiday in August was new to him.

"David's training to be a teacher."

"Is that true?" Billy asked. "My first wife was a teacher." It was hard to tell for certain if that was a good thing or not. David chose to remain silent.

"Long holidays."

David nodded. "Most teachers spend them preparing lesson plans for the next term."

There was a long silence. David found himself staring down at the grave, watching for movement. He assumed Helen was doing the same. In his camping chair, Billy was looking off into the distance as if he was recalling his first wife.

David regretted his decision to take up Billy's offer. They would have been better off going down to the car and getting a few hours' sleep. Sitting on a cold stone watching a middle-aged man silently reminiscing on his past didn't seem a productive way to spend the night. *I'll give him another five minutes, then I'll make an excuse and leave,* David decided. He was still trying to find a way to communicate his suggestion to Helen when Billy stood up.

Immediately David looked down at the grave but there was no sign anything had changed.

"Don't you ever want to help them get out?" David asked. He looked past Billy to the shovel propped up against the back of a gravestone.

"No."

The tone was pure horror, as if David had suggested the unspeakable. All he was considering was breaking up the soil a little to give the guy down there a hand. What harm could that do? And yet Billy acted like he had suggested offering up his mother as a sacrifice.

"You don't do that," Billy said. "You've seen the video?"

"The Chrysalids? Of course. Everyone's seen the video. It was passed around my school when I was about ten years old." Even now David could close his eyes and recall the bloody howl. The copy he'd seen was probably ten generations removed from the original footage, and the quality had deteriorated to such a point that it was hard to see anything between the white lines which sliced across the picture. Still, he had seen enough to understand.

"So why would you ever suggest . . . ?"

"But that was just once," Helen said.

Billy looked at her. She'd seen the video too? Of course she had – *everyone* had seen the video. It was up there with the Zapruder footage from Dealey Plaza or the images of the planes on 9/11. It was a part of everyone's collective memory.

"I had nightmares for weeks after watching that," David said.

"So you should."

Just the memory of the footage caused David's stomach to churn. A couple of friends had said they heard the risen man in the video speak, but the whole point about the video was that the man who was risen couldn't say anything. There was nothing left.

"It just seems so hard," Helen said. "After all that time underground they're expected to fight their way to the surface. Would it really be so terrible if we helped them out?"

"The Chrysalids video is the only answer you need to that; one of the risen with no ability to move or communicate or think. He just lay there until someone had the decency to cover him up again."

"Maybe it wasn't his time."

"It was," Billy said flatly."

"Then maybe that was just a one-off. There's nothing to say if you did it again you'd get the same result."

"Would you like to test that theory with your father?" Billy looked at both of them and harrumphed. "No, I thought not. Neither would anyone else. The Chrysalids proved that if you interfere in the process you damage the risen."

He waited for another argument from the pair of them. When there was nothing he relented. "No one wants to see their loved ones struggle. It's in our nature to try and help. But during a rising you have to push that nature aside, at least until the person has finished. Once they're up you can help them, that's exactly what we're here for, but until then you have to leave well alone. Got it?"

David nodded. He felt like Billy was treating the pair of them like schoolchildren. Maybe it was something he had picked up from his first wife.

"Just sit tight and wait. It won't be long now. And remember that whatever you see, there is nothing you can do to help me. Let me handle it."

"How many of these risings have you done?" Helen

asked to fill in the awkward silence after Billy had lectured them.

"Two thousand, one hundred and thirty-nine." He didn't have to stop and think. *The number must always be there,* David thought.

"I could talk you through each one of them."

"*All* of them?" Helen asked.

"You don't forget them, not if you care. It's an honour to spend time with the risen."

It sounded like the sort of insincere sales talk David had heard when he called around Family Directors, but he sensed Billy really meant what he said. For him it genuinely was a vocation rather than a job.

"Have you ever done anyone famous?"

"*Done* anyone famous?" Billy repeated, his deadpan delivery highlighting the crass nature of the question. "I've helped celebrities with their rising. Some of them even told me secrets any tabloid would pay handsomely to print. They do that, you know? Every few months I get a call asking if I want to write a book about my time as a Family Director. What they really mean is do I want to tell tales on all the people who entrust me with their secrets? Is that what you'd want for your father? That's why Nathaniel is such a danger. Not only does he not know what he's doing, but I fear that if he ever did learn something valuable, he would sell it at the first offer."

Billy cocked his head to one side. David heard a sound. He froze. Helen's hand on his arm squeezed tighter.

The sound was a low noise like two rocks being scratched together. Then came a groan. David had no doubt it came from Reginald Wooley.

David levered himself off the sarcophagus and carefully placed his feet on the ground. He didn't know how sound travelled below ground, whether each footstep would boom like thunder.

He took a step towards the grave. Billy was out of his chair. He held up one hand. *Stop!*

Helen flashed the torch across the surface of the grave. The white beam picked out rocks and clumps of dirt. A crack ran half the length of the grave.

Billy held his finger up to his lips. "Ssh." He took a step closer and then lowered himself to his knees. He put a flat palm out on the ground beside the headstone.

"He's coming."

CHAPTER 8

THE FAMILY DIRECTOR moved with a calm urgency. Reaching behind for the restraints, he set them on the ground beside him. He worked without speaking, without even looking up at David and Helen. He focussed solely on the patch of dirt in front of the headstone.

David stared at the ground. Looking to spot any movement. This was the moment when the video cameras invariably turned away. This was the mystery.

He heard Helen's heavy breathing beside him as her hand dug so deep into his arm her fingernails would leave scars. They were trapped in a no-man's-land; a couple of steps away from the edge of the grave, a few paces in front of the stone sarcophagus that had been their seat. They were frozen, half crouching, with no knowledge of whether to stay or retreat. David made a quick calculation; when Reginald Wooley rose, they would be within easy reach. The twenty-year-old corpse wouldn't know what he was doing. He wouldn't be responsible for anything that happened.

We should go back to safety, David thought. But he didn't move. Neither of them did.

A hand exploded from beneath the soil. Fingers grasped the air.

David screamed. Quietly, almost inaudible, but Billy glanced across before immediately returning his attention to Reginald Wooley.

A second hand rose from the grave. The nails on each finger were long, almost talons. The skin was streaked with dirt but beneath the superficial colouring, the man's skin was pale blue and pulled taut over bones like broken sticks.

Reginald Wooley pushed a pile of soil away from him and then scrabbled back to repeat the action. The mound that quickly grew on the surface of the grave reminded David of the hillocks in ploughed fields where badgers had been at work.

A drone reverberated through the ground, like an engine or a piece of mining machinery. After a moment David realised he was listening to Reginald Wooley's voice seeping up through the earth while he worked to free himself of his grave. David wondered whether the man had had the presence of mind to read the PoeWords printed on the underside of the coffin lid when he awoke: instructions which told the occupant not to panic and explained how to use the catches to unlock the coffin from the inside.

David wondered how his father would feel when the first movement triggered the pale light and he opened his eyes to find the salmon pink silk just a few inches in front of his nose. He didn't know his father well enough to guess if he would scream and shout and rail against awakening from twenty years lost in death, or whether he would calmly follow the instructions and burrow his way up to the surface.

Just how much do the dead really understand? he thought. He would have asked Billy but parked the question for later. The Family Director was poised above the grave with his hand still in the air calling for absolute silence.

The hands reaching out from the grave worked with purpose. Quickly the mound of black soil grew until it was about a foot high. David reached out for the torch, cupped his hand around the bulb, and switched it on so that diffuse pink light fell onto the ground around him. Billy glared at him but didn't signal that he should turn it off, and so slowly David removed his hand and angled the light across the grave.

There was a loud crack; the coffin lid breaking, David assumed. It was followed by a thud deep underground as the soil in the grave slumped downwards. Frenzied hands pushed aside clods of dirt. The low murmur of Reginald Wooley's voice grew louder. A roar sounded like a rockfall heard from miles away. David felt it in his chest, his stomach, his bones.

Billy shifted forward on his haunches. He placed a hand on the steel chain.

Reginald Wooley's fingers grasped the two sides of the grave. A flurry of dirt fell back into the hole. He roared as he pulled himself from the ground.

Ragged clothes hung from his body. The cloth was tattered and pitted with holes where insects had eaten through the material. The suit looked like it had been draped onto the frame of a skeleton, hanging in folds from the man's shoulders. In life Reginald must have been a large man, but twenty years in the grave had reduced him to bones wrapped in skin.

He turned his head in the direction of the light. David moved to turn off the torch. Hesitated. Reginald had no eyes. Only dark sockets where shadows gathered. It was like staring into a deep pit and having the hole stare back at you.

David felt Helen draw in a breath as she prepared to scream, and knew he had done the same. She was shivering. For David, it felt like his body had flushed with heat.

He heard the tendons in Reginald's neck creak as the man turned his head away from the torch. He seemed to be reading the inscription on his own headstone.

"Reginald Wooley," Billy called.

The dead man turned in the direction of the Family Director. The creak sounded like a bridge just before the steel cords snap.

Reginald Wooley stumbled out of the hole and placed a hand on the top of his headstone. His fingertips scraped against the hard stone. This close, he smelled faintly of dust; like a musty room that had just been opened to the sunlight. The atrophied cords of his muscles lay against his neck in thin lines, trapped between bone and skin.

"Do you know where you are?" Billy asked.

Reginald's jaw levered open. A sound like rushing wind came from his mouth.

He's trying to speak, David thought.

"I'm William Kane. Your family invited me to look after you." The man's voice was soft; a million miles away from the abrasive manner he had sometimes displayed to David during the last couple of hours.

Singular strands of grey hair clung to the bald pate of Reginald's head. They drifted in the night air like fronds pushed and pulled by the current of a river.

David saw the man in profile: deep crevasses ran along the curvature of his skull. His jawbone showed through beneath non-existent gums. There were no teeth in his head, just a row of holes where the teeth had once sat and David knew that on the bottom of Reginald Wooley's coffin he would find a handful of enamel nuggets gathered in a pile where he had laid his head.

Billy rose until he stood toe-to-toe with the dead man. Half-hidden behind his back was the restraint. He murmured low, too quiet for David to hear what he said. There was a sense it was the tone that was important, rather than the words. The calm measured cadence suggested Billy was here to help. There was no reason to worry. Reginald clawing his way out of the grave was just another part of living and dying.

Reginald Wooley raised both his hands. Yellowed, crooked fingernails jutted from his fingertips. He screamed, a cry loud enough to wake the dead themselves, and launched himself at Billy.

CHAPTER 9

FOR A DEAD MAN, Reginald Wooley moved fast. There was no suggestion Reginald planned the attack. His empty eye sockets peered in Billy's direction, but David thought that was sheer instinct. The dead man slashed wildly—left and then right, staggering forward like a punch-drunk boxer in the last rounds of a fight. He raked the air in front of Billy with his talons, stripping the darkness.

The dead man opened and closed his jaws, creating a constant clunk-clunk-clunk sound. Beneath the sound was the soft wheeze of Reginald's breath as he tried to speak.

David took a step forward.

"Stay back," Billy said without taking his eyes off the dead man. "I don't need any help." He leaned back to avoid the next swiping attack from Reginald's flailing hands and then stepped toward the man before he had a chance to recover from his reckless swing. There was a loud click of metal as Billy fixed the handcuffs around Reginald's wrists, ratcheting the mechanism to tighten it until the steel was snug against the bone.

Reginald raised his hands and overbalanced. In a

fluid motion Billy had the risen man turned around and pressed down into the chair, and without David understanding how it had happened, Reginald Wooley was sat down, wrists cuffed together, with another restraint across his chest to hold him in place.

The dead man writhed against the fastenings. He twisted his arms to try and escape the handcuffs. The chair's front legs lifted from the ground as high as ten centimetres before the weight of the man's body slammed it back into the dirt.

"Ididn'tneedtocompletethereportuntilthemeetingo nTuesdayandMarysaidshe'dbehomelatebecausethekid swerecomingupfromLondonandIcan'tseeand . . . " The dead man's jaws chewed the words as he spoke them. They came from his mouth in a low torrent so David could not understand what he was saying, except to know that somewhere within the rush of sound there was something which made sense, at least to Reginald.

The front legs of the chair rose from the ground once again. And like before, they crashed back down after attaining no more than a couple of centimetres of air. Reginald snapped his jaws in Billy's direction. The Family Director kept a safe distance back from the man. Just in case. He looked behind him, picked up his camping chair, and re-set it a few inches further away before lowering himself into the seat. He sat with his hands crossed in his lap, his head to one side.

The dead man flailed against the chair before finally fading into resigned defeat.

"Reginald Wooley," Billy said. The two words loud and clear.

The dead man looked at the Family Director. There could be no doubt he reacted to hearing his own name.

"You are Reginald Wooley." Billy's voice was calm but firm. "I am William Kane and I am your Director. I have been asked by Mary, your wife, and your children Hazel and Robert, to look after you and help you through your transition. Do you understand?"

Reginald Wooley chewed the air with his toothless bite. The thighs of his trousers were striped with mud where he raked his hands along the material. "Couldn'thearanythingCouldn'tseeanythingDon'tknow whereMaryhasgonehasMaryleftmeAlwaysthoughtthat shehadathingforJohnSingletondidsheleavemeforJohn Singletonwhowilllookafter . . . "

"Do you hear me?" Billy said loudly, interrupting the dead man's low level chuntering.

Reginald squealed. A high-pitched sound like a kettle boiling.

"Your wife, Mary, and your children Hazel and Robert asked me to care for you," Billy repeated.

"Mary."

"Yes, Mary."

"Mary," Reginald repeated. He turned his head in Billy's direction.

"And your children Hazel and Robert." The metal supports of the camping chair creaked as Billy leaned back.

"Hazelcan'tmakeitonSundaybecauseshe'sgottoflyo uttoBerlinforameetingbecausesheworksforacompanyy ouknowandtheyneedhertogoovertoGermanyandsorto uttheproduction . . . "

David found himself leaning forward to try and pull meaning out of the stream of noise coming from the dead man. It was like listening to someone speaking a foreign language. Occasionally he could pick out words—like Sunday and Berlin and Germany—but much of it was too fast, too low.

"That's right. Hazel works for a pharmaceutical company. She wasn't able to get back for your wife's birthday lunch as she was flown out at short notice."

The man kicked out. David noticed his shoes—the leather was dulled and covered with dirt and dust but underneath they looked as if they had been new when the undertaker had fitted them onto his feet.

"Couldn'thearanythingneedtocompletethereportJo hnSingletonMary . . . "

Billy rose from his chair and took a position beside Reginald's chair. Despite the cuffs and the straps, the Family Director took great care in choosing his position—slightly to the left and just behind Reginald's shoulder so the dead man would not be able to reach out and strike the man paid to care for him.

Billy placed a hand on the man's shoulder.

Reginald howled. It was a sound of rage and frustration and fear. It boomed across the cemetery. The dead man strained against the fastening across his chest. The black material pulled taut and seemed certain to rip apart. David noticed the dry skin around the man's wrists gathered together like folds in a bedsheet, revealing a glimpse of dry, white bone beneath.

The chair jumped as Reginald struggled to free himself. He snapped at Billy and turned his head far enough around it seemed the tendons in his neck might actually break. Billy took a measured step backwards to remain out of reach.

"Germany."

A single word. Clear. Through Reginald's ragged

breathing and his rotten organs; tongue, voice box. Reginald was forming words through sheer force of habit over biology.

"That's right. Hazel was in Germany."

"Mary."

"Your wife sends you her love." Billy hesitated, and David thought the man was deciding what he dared to say next. "You died."

The man's face twisted into a grimace David assumed to be grief. Despite the cemetery and the headstone, David wondered whether Reginald Wooley had understood his condition before that moment. Certainly, his response suggested that even if he had been suspicious, Billy's words had confirmed the truth for him.

"You were at home with your wife, Mary. It was a heart attack."

"Mary."

"Mary loves you."

"JohnSingleton."

Billy shook his head quickly. "Your wife loves *you*, not John Singleton. Your wife and your daughter, Hazel, and your son, Robert."

"Hazel. Germany."

"Yes. Hazel was in Germany. Robert was with you. Mary and Robert."

Reginald shuddered in the chair as if someone had passed a thousand volts through his body. His legs kicked out. His arms stuck straight out in front of him as he strained to escape his bindings. His spine arched away from the back of the chair.

Billy placed a hand on the dead man's shoulder. "It's okay. Everything is going to be alright," he said.

"Who's Robert?" Reginald asked.

"Your son."

"I don't have a son."

From his left, David heard Helen cry out. He wondered how Robert Wooley would have reacted if he had been at his father's rising and discovered he had been forgotten. Maybe Billy was right—perhaps it was best if family stayed away. It was too late for the realisation now. He shook the fear away; *my dad won't have forgotten me.* They only had five years together, but that would be enough.

Billy spoke calmly. "Reginald Wooley. You were loved by your wife Mary and your children Hazel and Robert. You can rest in peace now."

Slowly Reginald Wooley's body relaxed back into his seat.

Billy continued to whisper gently to the man. The only responses he received were single words, except for a burst of unintelligible nonsense similar to the rant Reginald had made when he first rose from the grave. After fifteen minutes—twenty minutes at the most—Reginald sat slumped in the chair, head dropped forward onto his chest so his jawbone scraped against his ribs.

"He's gone," Billy said.

"What?" David jumped down from his seat and moved closer to the chair. "He can't be."

Billy motioned in the direction of the body. "There's nothing there."

"But he was awake for such a short period of time," Helen said. "Is that it?"

The Family Director nodded. "It's a miracle, but it's such a brief miracle. The most I've ever experienced someone return for is an hour, but that was unusual."

"What's the point?" David asked.

"That's a very deep question for a Friday night. What *is* the point? Why are any of us here?"

"But why would someone lie dead for twenty years to wake up for such a small period of time," Helen said. "It just doesn't make sense."

"None of this makes sense, but that doesn't make it any less true. You saw the man. You heard him speak."

"But he didn't *say* anything," David said. Frustration choked his throat and made it difficult to speak. He moved closer to Reginald's body. The man was slumped in the chair and definitely looked like a corpse, but he had looked like that for the last twenty years. "How can you know for sure? Maybe he's just resting."

"Thirty years of experience tells me he's gone."

Billy turned his back on the body and went behind the grave to pick up the shovel.

"What about all of that?" David asked, pointing to the array of equipment carefully laid out on the tarpaulin. "Why bring all of that if you didn't need it?"

"Just in case."

Billy reached for the shovel and pushed the blade into the grave. "Are you going to help?"

No. Why should I help when you've taught me nothing? He was tempted to storm off into the dark, return to the side of his father's grave and continue the vigil. His father would be different. He would be alert, responsive. He would be able to answer all of the questions David had stored up for him since the moment he had first decided he would attend the rising.

What if he can't? David thought. The idea was clean panic. *What if after all this he can't speak. This is the only chance I have.*

He stood frozen beside the grave of Reginald Wooley even as Helen reached for the spade. She started to enlarge the hole where the dead man had burrowed up from his coffin.

David crouched down in front of the body. There was nothing to suggest Reginald had any life left within him. *That had been what he had looked like when they had buried him the first time*, but David knew he was desperately trying to find hope where there was nothing. Reginald Wooley was dead. Reginald Wooley had spoken his last words.

Ever.

CHAPTER 10

HELEN AND BILLY had already carved a deep hole by the time David backed away from the corpse and went over to the Family Director. "Do you want me to take over? There must be other things you have to do."

Billy climbed out of the shallow pit and held out the handle of the spade. David took the Family Director's place in the hole. Helen was only a few centimetres away from him, diligently hacking through the dirt and flinging it into the pile of spoil to one side of the grave. She didn't seem to notice he was there, or if she did, she didn't care.

"Hey!" David said. When he received no response, he tried a little louder and put a hand out to interrupt Helen as she plunged the shovel down into the black earth. "Are you alright?"

She looked up. Even in the gloom her tears were visible. David pushed his spade aside and held out his hands to embrace her. She fell into his arms and he smelled her sweat and traces of the scent from her shampoo. "It's going to be alright," he told her.

"No, it isn't." She spoke into his shoulder, her words muffled. Her voice was strained; a sound David was most familiar with from the times when they had an argument and were in the slow, tentative stages of making up.

"What is it?"

"I don't know. It's just . . . " Helen's voice hitched and her words dried up. David didn't need to see her face to know the tears had started to roll down her cheeks again. This was Helen. It was how she reacted to grief. He had seen it when she was reading *A Monster Calls* or *The Grapes of Wrath*. When they had attended the funeral of her aunt she had sobbed silently for hours, her body trembling as he held her.

She leaned away from him and used the back of her hand to wipe her eyes, even though it only had the effect of smearing grave dirt across her cheeks. She looked like a child playing soldiers with camo paint.

David felt his heart ache. It was like Helen had reached into his chest and squeezed his heart in her fist, hard enough to stop it from beating for a couple of seconds. *Love*. There was no other way to describe the feeling. He considered telling her, but it wouldn't help. She didn't need him getting soppy and romantic, she needed his help to get the grave dug and Reginald Wooley reburied so they could move on. They just needed the night to be over.

She caught him staring at her. "What?" Helen said.

"Nothing." He returned to his task; the sound of the shovel cutting through the soil masked his heavy breathing. Billy's well-developed muscles began to make sense; caring for those rising was more physical than David had appreciated.

They worked without talking; the activity punctuated by the sound of the shovel hitting the dirt and their laboured breathing. David wiped sweat from his brow but as soon as he did, it was replaced with more. Salt water dripped into his eyes and blinded his vision.

He was vaguely aware of the sides of the grave growing steeper as they burrowed down. Removing each load of soil became a greater effort—throwing it over the side instead of merely casting it behind him. There wasn't enough air left in his lungs for talk; everything was focussed on breathing, and each breath tasted of black soil as if he were eating the dirt in which Reginald had lain.

Helen found the coffin. The hard clunk as the metal blade scraped the wooden surface prompted David to turn. She looked up. In the gloom she was almost invisible, a vague shadow against the night.

"Is that . . . ?" David asked.

"I assume so."

David propped his spade against the side of the grave and dropped to his knees. His fingertips found the hard edge of the coffin lid and he began to push aside soil to clear the area.

The lid was canted at an angle. "Move to the side," he asked Helen. He pulled and the lid rose a few centimetres; still held down by the weight of the soil.

The grave became brighter and David looked up to see Billy standing above them, shining the torch into the hole. In front of him, Helen was covered in mud. Her jeans were dark brown instead of blue, her hair was streaked through with dirt. Her eyes peered out from a dirty face. She slipped a hand into the gap beneath the lid and scooped out a handful of dirt.

David manoeuvred himself within the confines of

the grave until he was crouched beside Helen. He grabbed hold of the coffin lid and together they prised it upwards.

"That's okay," Billy called down to them.

The silk lining of the coffin had faded to a milky blue. In places the material had shredded and the padding around the lid where the PoeWords were fixed had been torn. David tried not to imagine Reginald Wooley waking up with pale light washing over him as he tried to make sense of the writing so close to his face.

He tried not to imagine what it would be like for his father to do the same in just a few hours.

Mounds of black dirt lay across the bottom of the coffin, like small hillocks on a sandy beach. Reginald's outline was pressed into the floor of the coffin where the man had lain for twenty years. The silk was clearly impacted; it looked like a mould into which a child would pour plaster of Paris.

"Eyes up," Billy called. He stood peering down from the edge of the grave, his hands hooked into the armpits of Reginald Wooley. The man was lowered into the grave and David and Helen reached up to collect him.

It was like taking hold of a bag of sticks. David made sure to grab hold of the dead man's trousers so he didn't touch his desiccated skin. He noticed Helen doing the same, grasping Reginald's shoulders through the material of his jacket.

He could feel the weight—or rather, the lack of weight—of the body. David estimated Reginald probably weighed a couple of pounds; nothing more than that. The skin was dried out to parchment and the bones had lost all their mass. It explained how Billy had manoeuvred him so easily on his own.

They placed Reginald back into his coffin; the shape of the man no longer quite matching the impression on the floor of the casket. David considered straightening Reginald's legs to better fit the silhouette but chose to leave him alone. He was dead, best to allow him a little dignity instead of being pushed and pulled to fit a specific position.

Helen closed the lid and stood for a moment looking down at the faded brass plate etched with Reginald's full name. his date of birth, and date of death. David wondered what she was thinking. She almost seemed to be praying, although she had never laid claim to any religion before. He didn't interrupt, but stood in silence beside her, his hands clasped together.

He was conscious of Billy waiting patiently at the top of the grave, his round face peering down at them but saying nothing. Happy to wait as long as it took before moving on to the next stage.

Helen looked up, wiped away a tear from her eyes. "Okay."

"You sure?" David asked.

Helen nodded but said nothing further as if she didn't trust herself to talk without breaking down and sobbing.

What's that all about? David thought, but it was a question for another day. Standing in Reginald's grave and quizzing Helen on her emotional state did not seem a wise choice.

"You go first," David said. He didn't like the idea of leaving Helen alone in the grave, even if it was only for a couple of seconds. For once Helen didn't argue against the perceived act of chivalry. Billy reached down to help her up and David created a stirrup with his hands which enabled her to push up and drag herself out of the trench. David followed; throwing himself up and grabbing hold of Billy and Helen to haul himself to the surface.

"Do you two need a rest while I start filling it in?" Billy asked.

"If I sit down, I might never get up," Helen said. She reached for the shovel propped against the headstone and started pushing the mound of dirt onto the coffin. Thick clods landed on the wooden lid with heavy thuds. To David it sounded terribly permanent. He thought of the day they buried his father, imagining standing by the grave and listening to the sound after the service, although he would have been too young to remember it accurately.

"How would you have done all this on your own?" Helen asked.

"You manage. Good help is hard to get. Most people stick it out a week or two." Billy shrugged. "In the end you give up trying to find anyone. We help each other out when we can."

"We?"

"The other Directors in the cemetery. If I've got a few hours before my own client is rising and I see someone finishing I often go over and give them a hand. And then others do the same in return. We get by."

"I didn't see anyone rushing to your help tonight," David said.

"They knew you two were here."

David wasn't sure how to take that remark. The cemetery was still. Silent. He didn't like the idea of all those Family Directors sitting on their camping chairs in the darkness and following what was happening at Reginald Wooley's graveside. In the end he decided there was nothing to scrutinise—he and Helen had been there, it was a fact, nothing more sinister than that.

Fatigue washed through his bones and sapped the strength from his muscles. Just lifting the spade was hard. His arms felt like they had weights tied around the wrists. Pain flashed along his shoulders like lightning strikes.

"What time is it?" he asked, but struggled to understand the answer Billy gave. It felt like the night had already lasted forever. Like he was living in a world of perpetual darkness.

Between the three of them, they scraped the dirt until it lay over the coffin, creating a small mound. "It will settle in time," Billy told them. "Six months from now it will have levelled out and then the family can decide what they want to do—put a concrete plug over the grave or just leave it as it is."

David staggered back to the sarcophagus and sat back down. He stared into the distance, too tired even to think. Helen joined him and they leaned against each other, shoulder to shoulder.

"Are you okay?" he asked her.

She nodded, and he felt her whole body rock with the response. "I thought it would be different. I thought . . . " and then she fell silent, and David didn't have the energy to ask her what she had expected.

David felt his grip on consciousness slipping

millimetre by millimetre. He opened his lips to say something to Helen—not even sure what he wanted to tell her, but the effort was too great and his slurred speech sounded like the sort of pronouncement Reginald Wooley had made when he came out of the ground. The observation scared David, but the fear floated away from him.

The scream woke him. Woke them both. It felt like rising up from the depths of a deep lake only to emerge into a black ocean of terror.

CHAPTER 11

WHILE THEY HAD slept Billy had covered them both with a blanket, and as David quickly came awake the material wrapped itself around him and seemed to hold him fast.

He was slow to move. Because of the blanket, because of the deep ache in his limbs. He jerked in response to the scream and was immediately aware of Helen propped against him.

The sky was pale crimson as if it had been washed in blood. The cemetery was laid out in front of him. The haphazard collection of headstones promised order from chaos if he could just understand the pattern. Dotted between the grey headstones were small camps—black dome tents or occasionally just a solitary figure with no visible equipment around them.

Down in the car park, the number of cars was roughly the same. David could spot his own truck parked towards one end of the row of jeeps and SUVs—standing out because it was not black and it was the only vehicle which was not a Range Rover or an SUV.

Looking around the site of Reginald Wooley's grave it was clear Billy had cleared up and was long gone.

David couldn't explain why he felt disappointed. The man was a professional. He did exactly as he was paid to do.

Still, the absence of the small man hurt. The area around Reginald's gravestone was picked clean. It occurred to David that apart from the mound of dirt in front of the headstone, the only evidence Billy had even been there was the green blanket wrapped around them.

The scream . . .

He couldn't hear it now. There was just a memory, like an echo. Weak enough for him to question whether he had really heard the sound at all or if it had simply leaked out from a dream he couldn't remember.

"I think it came from over there," Helen said, her voice lazy with sleep. She pointed a hand towards an area that represented almost a third of the cemetery.

"You're awake."

"I think so," Helen said. "At least I hope so, otherwise this is a really tedious dream."

"Or nightmare," David said.

"A really pathetic nightmare. It can't even conjure up a functioning zombie in a graveyard full of the rising dead."

"Don't use the Z word."

The scream sounded again. David turned in the direction of the sound. Beside him, Helen stood up and peered through the morning mist.

There was no obvious source of the noise. *But then what was I expecting, an arrow pointing down from the heavens?* David thought.

"Over there," Helen said.

David followed her gaze. A man was running

between the headstones. After a couple of seconds David spotted a second man working his way down the stone steps from a tent at the very crest of the hill. Both men were dressed in the standard black suit of Family Directors.

"Someone's rising gone awry?" David asked. The noise sounded too human to be one of the dead. He could never imagine Reginald making a sound like that. There was too much energy in it. Too much life.

"We're going?" Helen asked, and then as she stood up David realised it wasn't a question, it was a statement of fact. She had taken three paces before David had even managed to stand. She paused to calculate the most direct route from where they were to the spot where the sound was coming from, and then angled down three rows of headstones to connect with a path that led to a stone staircase.

"Slow down, I'll break an ankle," David called as he stumbled over the ground. He reached out for the stone wings of an angel to stop himself from pitching forward.

If Helen heard him she paid no attention. She reached the staircase and started to climb. Twenty feet up, the staircase connected with another of the rugged paths that criss-crossed the cemetery and by the time she reached that she was halfway to their destination.

David paused to catch his breath. He spied another two figures converging on the same spot. Four professionals, and the two of them. Six people rushing into whatever peril the scream indicated.

The sound cut out and the silence that followed was more ominous than the scream itself.

The destination was a grey tent. They approached

from the wrong angle to see what was waiting for them. David heard the crunch of gravel under his feet and the rough breathing as he raced into the fray. He followed Helen between the headstones.

She stopped just short of the tent and David squeezed to stand beside her. Ahead of them was an open grave, the dark earth scattered recklessly around the plot as if the occupant had exploded from the ground. Clumps of mud clung to the headstone, obscuring the name of the occupant. There was a broken chair, the frame reduced to firewood. Equipment was scattered around the ground and David felt he could read the story in the scene: the dead person had risen and whoever had tried to restrain them had failed. It happened; he'd read about it; sometimes the dead were so filled with rage when they awoke that it was difficult to care for them. In this case, the restraints had failed and so the dead person was unfettered. David thought about Reginald Wooley's sharp nails and gnashing toothless jaw. Despite the frailty and weakness, rage could power a lot of damage in a body like that.

So where are they?

Helen walked past the grave to the grey tent. Swathes of black tape covered the surface, but despite the repairs David doubted it was waterproof.

When David walked around the tent he found the four Family Directors. They stood with their backs to him, blocking his sight of whatever had screamed. Helen approached and one of them whirled around, a baseball bat raised, ready to swing.

"Hold on," Helen said. The man paused.

"What are you doing here?"

"We heard the screams. We came to help."

One of the others turned around. *Billy.*

"It's okay, they're with me," he said.

The man with the baseball bat looked unconvinced but he lowered the weapon and stepped aside to let Helen and David join the circle.

In front of them, one of the dead lay on the ground. A handcuff dangled from her wrist and David noticed two fingers missing from the other hand, although it was impossible to know if that had happened in the grave or when someone had tried to restrain the woman.

She wore a faded yellow dress covered in fresh crimson blood. The hand with the handcuffs had long nails. Two of them were broken. All of them were covered in blood that spread up her wrist and her arm like a glove. A black band fastened her arms to her sides.

She lay curled on her side. David thought she had probably died her second death, but from the look of carnage around her she had gone down fighting.

"What happened?"

"Amateur," Billy said, and at first David thought the criticism was aimed at him.

Further back from the grave he noticed two more Family Directors, the tails of their black suit jackets trailing in the mud. As he paid more attention to the scene, he realised their attention was focused on something in front of them. He stepped around the curled figure of the dead woman, careful to remain beyond her reach in case she should suddenly come to life. On the ground, in a shape not dissimilar to the dead woman, was a man in a tattered black suit. The material was ripped. Smatters of blood stained the cloth—almost black rather than red.

He was silent. To David that did not seem to be a good sign. The two Family Directors had a first aid kit open between them and they were emptying most of the contents onto the man; wrapping him in bandages and pouring iodine over the cream gauze to turn it brown.

Nathaniel. David recognised him from the crop of dark hair and the state of his clothes.

David stepped around the two Family Directors. There was a sense of voyeurism in his action, but he felt it was important he understood what had happened to Nathaniel. This was the man who had offered to guide them for a fee, a man who had portrayed himself as experienced. This was what happened if you tried to help someone through a rising and you didn't know what you were really doing.

"It happens," Billy said. He stood so close that the warmth of his breath brushed against David's cheek when he spoke.

"What? How?"

"You saw Reginald; he was mild. But sometimes they come out of the ground confused and angry and panicked and that can be a deadly combination of emotions. Usually, the dead are too weak to inflict any real damage, but occasionally they have enough about them to be lethal. It's why we're here, as much to protect everyone else as to have a gentle rising."

"And Nathaniel? He was unlucky?"

"No. He was unprepared and a chancer." There was real heat in Billy's words. "It was always going to happen to Nathaniel. He had no one to blame but himself."

"Sounds harsh."

"I told him he should leave the cemetery. He was preying on vulnerable people and he wasn't safe. If I'd had my way he would have been run out of here months ago."

"I can see why you didn't agree with us coming here."

"You're different. I don't think people should be allowed to manage a rising if they're not trained, but that's because it isn't safe. But you came to the cemetery for the right reasons. You came to pay respects."

I came for information, David thought. He felt guilty at Billy's assumption that his motivation was honourable. *If I already knew what happened to dad, would I just have handed over the money for a professional to take care of him?* It was impossible to know for certain. He wanted to believe he would still have the desire to look after his father himself, to make sure he had the best care, but in truth, he would never know.

"Is he going to be okay?"

"No," Billy said.

"But he will get better?" Helen asked.

"There's nothing we can do for him but put him out of his misery."

"You're going to kill him?" David was aware his voice rose as he asked the question.

Billy didn't answer. He watched the two Directors in silence as they worked on Nathaniel's body. Binding and treating it. *What for?* David wanted to ask. *Are you just pretending to care for him?*

One of the Directors turned around and looked up. "Can you pass me my bag?" she asked.

A woman? She was dressed in the same dark suit and tie. Her hair was pulled tightly back against her head.

The man with the baseball bat peeled away from the group. A moment later he hurried back with a black Gladstone bag that looked like a doctor's case from the 1920s. Scuffed leather and dull metal clasp. The woman found a small bottle and she placed it on the ground beside her. A moment later she located a syringe and removed the sheath protecting the point. She sucked liquid from the bottle into the syringe with practised ease.

"We're agreed?" she asked.

"Yes," the others said. Even Billy, David noticed.

"You can't do this."

"Shut up," Billy snapped.

"This is murder." David tried to direct his words to the woman holding the syringe, but she didn't hear him. Instead, Billy grabbed him by the waist and bulldozed him back ten paces before David had a chance to resist. Even once he understood what was happening he couldn't fight back against the tight package of muscle which Billy represented.

He punched Billy in the face. The man did not flinch. He hit him in the chest. The stomach. The man continued to push him away from the syringe.

"This is wrong," David said. His arms flailed at Billy as he tried to find a way to fight the Family Director.

"No, it isn't," Helen said. She had followed the pair and stood a short distance away. "It's horrible, and terrible, but it's the right thing to do."

"How do you know?" David asked.

"Listen to your wife."

"She's not my wife." The words came out harsher than David had intended and Helen looked like she'd been slapped. "I'm sorry. I didn't mean . . . "

"I know what you meant," Helen said.

"If we don't do this then Nathaniel will die. Slowly. Painfully. The woman did too much damage to him and we're an hour away from the nearest hospital. He will die whatever we do."

"You expect me to believe that?"

"I don't care what you believe. I'm just telling you the facts. You chose to do whatever you want with them."

"You hated him."

Billy shook his head. "No. I hated what he did. I hated the way he preyed upon the bereaved. I hated how he cheapened our profession. But I didn't hate Nathaniel. He was good fun. When you had a long night on vigil he'd come down for a chat and he could make you laugh until tears ran down your face."

There was a real sense of loss in Billy's words as if in remembering Nathaniel he realised the man was not coming back. "When it's cold and dark and you're sitting on your own at the side of a grave he was a good guy to keep you entertained."

Behind Billy, the woman stood up. Her work was done.

CHAPTER 12

AS BILLY RETURNED to join his colleagues, David waited with Helen. "Are you okay?" he asked.

"No. Are you?"

He shook his head. "I didn't think it would be like this. I thought it would be . . . "

"Easy?"

"Not quite." He was stung by the judgement in her words.

"I said it would be hard. I said you didn't need to come."

"I know." Helen's short response was loaded with feeling and David didn't think he could navigate her emotions.

"You can wait down in the car if you want."

She laughed. Hard. Short. As if the very idea was offensive. "I don't plan to run away."

"Sorry, I didn't mean . . . "

He fell silent, not entirely sure he knew what he did mean by the suggestion. They stood side by side, but not together, and watched as the crew of Family Directors went about the task of tidying away their murder. It occurred to David that if there was one profession suited to the role of hiding a murder, it was them. They broke down Nathaniel's battered tent and collected the few pieces of equipment into a small pile. They gathered around Nathaniel's body, and it looked like they were doing *something*, but it was hidden from David's view and he was sure that was not accidental. He assumed they were making sure Nathaniel did not rise up in twenty years' time to accuse them of his murder.

From behind the wall of black suits he heard a wet sound. *What are they doing?* He stepped forward but Helen put a hand on his arm and shook her head. "They don't want you to see them."

She was right. Still, he shirked Helen's hand away from his arm and pressed forward. He was two steps away from the Family Directors when Billy turned.

"What are you doing to him?" David asked.

"This is nothing to do with you."

David took a step forward. Behind Billy, the Family Directors had drawn together to hide Nathaniel's body from view.

"You're tired and you're scared and you're making a bad decision," Billy said. "Just let it go."

"You killed him, and now you're trying to stop him from rising."

Billy nodded.

"That's wrong."

"Wrong and right are fluid ideas. You come to understand that when you sit beside people at their rising and listen to them talk. Maybe your father won't have anything to say to you, but sometimes with the rising they lose their filter. Their inhibitions go and they say everything they wanted to say when they were alive. We're like priests for the dead; listening to their confessions. Hearing the secrets they've allowed to fester for decades. There's nothing good about a rising. Nothing to be celebrated. It's the last gasp of someone; full of foetid air."

"Then maybe you should get another job?" David said. "Do something you think is worthwhile."

Billy smiled. Shook his head. "This job *is* worthwhile. It's essential. It's just not a good job if you understand. It's something I *need* to do instead of something I *want* to do."

Behind Billy, the female Family Director turned around. "It's done," she said over her shoulder. The small group drifted apart to reveal Nathaniel lying on the tarpaulin in the middle of the grave. David couldn't see what they had done to silence him. Too late he realised Billy had been distracting him to give the others a chance to finish their work.

"I'll go and tell . . . " David said. He realised he sounded like a child complaining in a school playground. The recognition made him even more angry—as if the others had manipulated him. "You have to pay for what you've done."

"We accept our responsibility," the woman said. "We should have stopped Nathaniel when he arrived months ago. He's dead because of us and we accept that. But I don't believe we were wrong to end his pain. That was the humane thing to do."

David didn't have a response. Maybe spending so much time with the dead caused the Family Directors to forget the value of life. He glared at the woman, and then at Billy. He had thought the squat man was . . . if not a friend, then at least someone he respected. Now he discovered the Family Directors were just as he had originally thought—ghouls, preying on the vulnerable.

He turned away and marched down the hill. "I'm going back to the truck," he said to Helen as he passed her, but he was aware she didn't join him. He walked down the hill alone, unlocked the front door of the truck, and slumped behind the steering wheel. He pushed away the urge to start the engine and drive out of the cemetery, leaving his father's rising to nature. Instead, he sat and glared up the hillside where, dotted amongst the graves, Helen conspired with the Family Directors.

CHAPTER 13

DAVID HAD HIS eyes closed but he was not asleep when Helen opened the passenger door. He said nothing, and in response she sat in the passenger seat and closed the door behind her. Silence settled between them like black snow. David peered out at the hillside. With the daylight, he could see rows of headstones like brittle teeth, and dotted between them were the tents of the Family Directors as they waited for the twenty-year anniversaries to roll around and for the dead to rise.

He checked the clock on the dashboard. It was almost seven. He had a couple of hours before he needed to return to his father's graveside and help him through his rising. His stomach churned at the thought.

"I asked them to help us," Helen said eventually.

He didn't know what he was supposed to say to her. He'd already made it clear he didn't want anything to do with those vultures, even though it meant handling his father himself. Even though he now understood how unprepared he was for the event.

"They refused."

There was very little movement on the hills of the

cemetery. Occasionally a bird would scratch against the pale blue sky. The trees shifted slightly in the wind. But the cemetery itself looked dead.

"Are you listening to me?" Helen asked.

"Yes."

David started to read the names on the row of gravestones closest to the car. Matthew Haynder. Francis Wilkes. Xian Hunter. The writing on the surfaces was faded. Some of the graves were impossible to decipher. A stone angel was missing the tip of a wing. The corner of Matthew Haynder's memorial stone had broken away. The dates on all of the graves identified that they had been there for decades, some of them reaching close to a century. All of the occupants were long risen.

"Annie said you were right."

"Annie?" David asked.

"The woman up on the hill. The Family Director."

You were talking about me behind my back? David thought, but said nothing. He was tired and his brain fizzed like an electrical switch with a loose wire, but still he had enough presence of mind not to accuse Helen of conspiring against him. They already had enough fuel for the argument simmering beneath their words without searching for anything new.

"We had a long talk. She said it's a common mistake. You want to do the right thing by your family and the most obvious way is to come to their rising, but it's almost always a mistake. It's too raw. Too personal."

The second row of gravestones was harder to read. It was like the test in the opticians. The graves were of a similar age—none less than fifty years old. David assumed the graveyard had filled up from the bottom and that as he went up through the rows the graves would become more recent. Planning graveyards to ensure whole rows of the dead did not rise on the same day must be a relatively recent technique.

"I'm sorry," Helen said. "Do you want me to leave?"

His first instinct was to agree. He assumed Helen had made the offer even though she knew there was no way she could follow through. What would she do, walk back twenty miles along that narrow road? Wait until Billy or Annie or one of the others finished and ask them for a lift back to civilisation? She couldn't leave. They both knew that. David felt like he was being wrapped into a small box. Tied tighter and tighter so he couldn't move. So tight he no longer had any choice over what was happening to him.

Go on then.

It would serve her right. She had insisted on coming despite everything he said to her. Now she was trying to manipulate him by pretending to apologise. Well, he would show her.

David glanced across the cab. She'd been crying. He understood the offer was genuine. If he told her he truly wanted to be alone she would get out of the truck and start walking.

"Please stay," he told her. "I'm sorry for being so foul."

"Don't apologise. Annie explained. She sees it every time a member of the family insists on being present at a rising."

Annie explained. David wanted to snap at Helen and her new best friend, but maybe there was something in what the Family Director had said. After all, she was the expert.

"She told me she wanted to help us but she was already committed to a client. They all said the same."

"Even Billy?" David asked. He wasn't sure why he felt betrayed that the man had refused to help. After all, the guy was on a payroll, and he'd said all along that he wasn't available. He would have refused any help they offered him, so it was unreasonable that he should be irritated by them, but David couldn't change how he felt.

"Annie spent some time talking to me while she was waiting for her rising. She offered to let me stay but I told her we'd already watched Billy assist Reginald so there probably wasn't much else I could learn. And anyway, I was conscious I'd been away from you for too long. I didn't want you to think you'd been abandoned."

David cast a glance across the cab at Helen. Did she know that was exactly what he had been thinking?

"She loaned me her stethoscope," Helen said, pulling the medical instrument from her pocket. "And she showed me how to use it by letting me listen to her own client. I won't be anything like as accurate as Annie or Billy, but at least it will give us some idea of how your father is progressing."

"Thanks," David said.

"She said we should get some sleep. We don't have long, but she said any rest we get now will make a big difference." Helen paused and glanced across the cab, meeting David's gaze for the first time since she had come down from the hill. "That is, if you want me to help. If not, I can stay in the cab. I just think . . . "

"That would be great," David said. The tension in the cab lessened. It was still there, like a bitter aftertaste, but the sense they were about to launch into another argument had passed.

"Thanks," Helen said. To David's ear she sounded genuinely grateful. He couldn't understand. He was here because his father was rising. He *had* to be there. He'd handed Helen a get-out-of-jail-free card and yet when he told her she could come with him to the grave she was relieved. She'd seen what had happened with Reginald and Nathaniel. She knew what the risks were. *If I were you, I'd run for the hills*, David thought. And then he looked at the hill directly in front of him, with the graves scattered around, and laughed at the idea.

"What's so funny?" Helen asked. There was an edge to the question as if she feared she was the butt of the joke.

"Nothing," David said, and when he could see from her scowl that his response was not going to be enough, he pointed through the window. "I was thinking we're both mad. We should be running for the hills. And then I saw what was in the hills and . . . " his voice trailed away and he shrugged.

Helen smiled; the joke didn't warrant a laugh.

"You need to rest. Annie's orders." David smiled to show all was forgiven.

"You too."

"You're right." He closed his eyes even though he knew there was no possibility of sleeping. His nerves fired every time he heard a sound outside the cab. His heart raced. He tried to slow his breathing to something approaching normality, but it was too shallow, too fast. There was no chance he'd fall asleep, however hard he tried. It was like standing outside the school hall just before a test, everything he'd learned racing through his head.

Helen's breathing grew louder and he peeked across the cab. Sleep had drained the stress from her features. She looked just like she had the day they had met. His heart lurched. Was it love? He still didn't know for sure. It was . . . something. An emotion he had never truly experienced before.

"Just don't fuck it up," he muttered to himself.

The springs of the truck's seat creaked as he shifted position. He made a pillow out of his jacket and pressed it against the side window. For a while he stared out of the window, watching the stillness of the cemetery from his slightly tilted angle. He started counting gravestones, back from one hundred.

Ninety-nine. Ninety-eight. Ninety-seven.

There was no chance he could fall asleep, but even so, he closed his eyes and visualised the rows of gravestones and continued to count down.

Ninety-six. Ninety-five.

He tried to remember exactly what Billy had done when Reginald Wooley had risen from the ground. The Family Director had snapped the handcuffs onto one wrist and then quickly fastened him to the chair. The act had been done with a smooth familiarity that spoke of years of experience. It had been as easy for Billy as it would have been for David to enter a classroom full of seven-year-olds. Easier.

Ninety-one? Damnit! Ninety. Eighty-nine. Eighty-eight.

Billy was right—this was a job for the professionals, but it was too late to do anything about that now. He could hardly ask his father if he wouldn't mind just holding on for a day or two until he could make arrangements. *I mean, it's not as if I didn't have twenty years to plan for today,* David thought.

Eighty-two?

He opened his eyes. The scene outside the cab had not changed. He thought of the Family Directors sequestered in their tents. *I bet they'll be getting their beauty sleep,* David thought. He tried not to be bitter; it was his decision not to get a professional. A stupid decision, but his and his alone. Now he just had to deal with that and not try and blame anyone else for his mistake.

He checked the time on the dashboard clock. Seven-thirty. He'd go up to the grave in half an hour. There was no point sitting and waiting if he wasn't going to get any rest. Half an hour would give Helen at least some respite, and hopefully, an hour after that it would all be over and he could get on with his life.

Not that I'll ever tell mum about this.

He closed his eyes, *Seventy-Nine, Seventy-Eight, Seventy-Seven,* and waited for his father to rise.

CHAPTER 14

THE TAP ON the glass woke David. It was as much the sensation as the noise. David's head rested against the window and it felt like the tapping burrowed directly through his skull into the deepest part of his brain.

He sat upright. Billy was standing outside the truck. The Family Director wore his black tie perfectly knotted. Dark shadows rimmed his eyes. His skin was pale as if he had not seen sunlight in weeks.

"It's happening. You need to hurry."

David's eyes flicked down to the clock on the dashboard. "It's only eight o'clock. You said . . . "

"I was wrong," Billy said simply. "There's no point arguing about that now. You've got about twenty minutes to get up and be ready before he breaks through."

Beside him, he was aware of Helen waking up. She stretched her arms out and pressed her hands flat against the glass of the windscreen. "I didn't oversleep," David told her quickly.

"But you did get some sleep?" Helen asked.

"A little." The admission sounded like a confession of guilt. If he'd been serious about his father's rising he should not have been able to sleep at all. The fact that he had nodded off—even if it was just for ten minutes—was a betrayal.

"Good," Helen said. She meant it. He could tell she wasn't just saying it to make him feel better. "You owe it to your dad to be as ready as you can be."

He nodded. "I love you," he said. The words took him by surprise.

Helen smiled. Wide. Despite the fatigue in her face, her eyes flashed with joy. "I love you too, even though you can be a miserable bugger, David Chadwick."

The knock on the glass was louder the second time. Billy glared at them through the window. "Get a move on, he isn't going to wait," Billy called, but despite the surly content of the words, he almost smiled. Almost. David wanted to assume the sentiment was there but the Family Director was simply too tired to act upon it.

He scrabbled for the door handle and let himself out, falling from the truck onto the hardpan of the cemetery's car park. Billy turned and was heading toward the hill before David had recovered his balance.

David waited for Helen to come around the front of the truck and together they struck out for the grave. His legs felt like ribbons. The morning sun scratched the back of his eyes. He stretched to push the aches out of his muscles but it had no effect. His mind felt like it was running at half-speed.

Billy was halfway up the hill when he turned to windmill his arm to encourage them to catch up. David peered past the small man and tried to spot his father's grave. He knew the rough location but even in the daylight, there was nothing to differentiate one row of graves from the next.

Billy started moving again before they had caught up with him. He took the steps two at a time. *How does he do that?* David wondered, but he conserved his breath to focus on climbing. He stared down at the uneven steps just in front of his feet and was only vaguely aware of Billy further up the hill. Even so, the sense of urgency communicated by the Family Director encouraged David to push harder to get to the top.

Soon, he thought. There were times over the last decade when it felt like he had been crawling towards this moment. During the last year, the days had passed so slowly he sometimes felt it would never arrive. Buried deep within him had been the suspicion that something would prevent his father from rising. Or prevent him from being present at the rising. Those fears were gone. Now it was happening.

He reached his father's grave, out of breath and with grey spots pricking his vision.

"You okay?" Helen asked.

He nodded. It was all he had the energy to do. He couldn't believe she was able to talk after the climb.

"Spin classes," Helen said. He caught her looking along the line of graves to where Billy stood impatiently by the headstone.

"I'll catch up," he wheezed.

She took a step toward Billy and then stopped. "I'll wait. We go together."

Fatigue washed over him like a wave. He wanted to curl up and sleep for a week. Failing that, a strong espresso would at least jolt him out of the worst of the tiredness.

Helen led the walk along the uneven path between

the graves, her hand trailing behind her. He felt the adrenalin kick in. It churned his empty stomach but cleared his head so at least he could think.

Billy was kneeling on the concrete surround and leaning over the grave.

David waited until the Family Director straightened up and removed the stethoscope from his ears. "I thought you couldn't help?"

Billy shrugged. "I figured you could do with a hand."

"How far gone is he?" Helen asked.

"He'll be here soon."

Soon? David wanted to ask. *What's soon? In the next minute? Five? Ten?* He dropped to his knees beside the grave and placed his hand flat on the ground. He thought he could feel dirt moving beneath his fingers. *This is happening.*

He knelt at the side of the grave, his hand resting lightly on the surface. Helen took up a position beside him; both of them on the far side from Billy who continued to stare down into the packed earth as if he were watching Graham Chadwick claw his way to the surface.

David felt a tremble beneath his fingertips. He looked at Helen and then across at Billy. The Family Director gave a short nod of his head. *It's time.* He stood and walked behind the grave and came back with the heavy chair David had last seen set beside the headstone of Reginald Wooley. Obviously, while he and Helen were sleeping in the truck Billy had lugged his own equipment to the grave.

Billy settled himself into the small camping chair and spent the time checking the array of equipment.

RICHARD FARREN BARBER

The tools were laid out alongside the edge of the grave. David recognised most of them from the hours he'd spent on websites preparing for his trip to Gilroes cemetery, but there were a few strange items, which he assumed were either highly specialised or Billy's own design.

David heard the sound of fingernails scratching against stone. *Dad.* He visualised the man based on the only photograph he possessed. The man underground would look nothing like the image he carried—the blue eyes that peered out from the photograph would be gone. His skin would be grey and tough as leather. David tried to stem the rising sense of excitement which flooded through his body.

"Dad," he whispered. He wiped a tear from his eyes. It was ridiculous to be so emotionally attached to an idea.

"He might not . . . " Helen started to say but he shrugged her touch away.

"He will," David said. He noticed the look that passed between Helen and Billy. Well, they could both go straight to hell. This was his father. He was going to be okay. He *had* to be. It wasn't going to be like any of the horror tales they told where the person rose up with half his face eaten away because there had been a crack in the casket which had allowed all manner of insects to pour in and feast on the body. It wasn't going to be a rising where the person didn't remember who they were and said nothing—or worse, where they spent their final few minutes screaming and raging against the solidity of death. Or cursing their families and spewing decades of repressed hate.

It was his father. The rising would go as planned. Everything would be perfect.

TWENTY YEARS DEAD

David leaned over to get closer, his cheek almost touching the dirt. This close he could smell the meaty smell of the earth. Each time he breathed in it was like he was down there in the ground with his father, the pair of them working together to claw free of the soil and breathe fresh air.

The surface of the grave trembled. Small chunks of earth rolled away to the edges. A hand rose up through the grave and snatched at the air.

CHAPTER 15

DAVID FORGOT TO BREATHE.
The air filled with the low murmur of his father's voice, but it was impossible to understand what the man was saying. Yet.

The skin on the back of his father's hand was stained with dirt and one of the long fingernails had broken. His father pushed a clump of dirt away and then a second hand appeared and the hole widened. The two hands scrabbled to push more dirt clear and David imagined his father struggling to breathe. He moved to reach forward and help but felt Helen's hand on his arm stay his progress. He recalled what Billy had said and remembered the Chrysalids. Maybe it wouldn't cause any harm if he helped his father to free himself of the grave. But *maybe* wasn't good enough.

The sound of fingernails scratching as they carved a way out of the grave sounded like mice skittering behind floorboards. David shuddered at the sensation. All he could do was sit there and listen and wait.

Between one heartbeat and the next, he watched his father slowly emerge from the grave. He saw the pale white of his skull push through the dirt; the perfectly coiffured hair in the photograph replaced with a few wire-like strands that lay across the bone. A black beetle skittered over the scalp and scurried into the dirt.

His father pulled himself up from the ground. Still, David felt the weight of Helen's hand upon his arm and the urge to rush forward and help was held in check for a little longer.

"Dad?" he whispered.

The man crawling out of the grave did not respond. He emerged with his back to David; a cracked egg of a head complete with thin fractures across the skin. The linen of his white shirt had rotted as he lay on the silk cushions of the coffin.

David's father muttered something unintelligible, and David felt a punch in his chest. *He's speaking nonsense.* It was always a possibility, maybe even a probability, but he had refused to consider it might happen. Whatever magic allowed the dead to rise up from their graves after twenty years was mercurial; it scattered its gifts randomly. David punched his fist into the ground at the unfairness.

His father turned slowly. The creak of his tendons as he twisted his neck around sounded like ropes pulled tight on a sailing ship. A green stain of lichen smudged his cheek. He blinked; eyelids shuttering empty holes.

"Dad?" David said quietly. He peered at the man to determine whether there was any reaction. There was nothing.

"Graham. Graham Chadwick," Billy announced. His voice boomed across the grave.

The man rising from the coffin turned to face the Family Director. His muscles creaked as they worked.

It was slow. Painful. Like watching a stop-motion video.

"You are Graham Chadwick. I am William Kane and I am your Director."

Graham Chadwick opened his mouth to speak. And hissed.

He pulled himself free from the grave. Dirt fell into the hole. Graham Chadwick crawled across the ground. He tried to rise to his feet but was unable to maintain his balance and crashed down onto his knees. The crunch of bone upon bone was the loudest sound in the graveyard.

He placed a hand on his own headstone and hauled himself into a standing position. Fingernails scraped against the stone surface. When Billy approached him, the dead man swung his arm as if trying to swat away his son.

"Graaaham," the man said. He lurched away from his grave, pushing off against the headstone.

Billy stepped back. He cast a quick look behind him and David assumed he was measuring the distance to his equipment before he made a move. Graham Chadwick launched himself at the Family Director. His hands splayed wide. Long fingernails raked Billy's face and drew thin lines of blood on his cheeks.

Billy batted away the man, pushing Graham so he fell.

"No!" David shouted. His father lurched over the uneven surface of the grave, stumbling across the divots of earth, hands scrabbling to reach the headstone and stop his fall. Instead, he landed on his back.

"He moves quickly for a dead man," Billy muttered.

He reached behind him for the handcuffs, but Graham was already on his feet again.

"Watch out," David said and jumped forward to wrap his hands around his father. Touching the man felt like an electric shock passing through his body. He felt his father's bones under his fingertips. His cheek pressed against his father's jacket and he breathed in the smell of twenty years of dust and decay.

"Dad, stop it. We're trying to help," David said.

The dead man did not react. It was impossible to know if he didn't hear, didn't understand, or just didn't care. He tried to haul his body in the direction of the Family Director. Despite the years in the ground and the wasted muscles, he possessed immense strength and David was only able to slow the man's progress.

His father stopped struggling.

At last. David loosened his grip.

Graham Chadwick turned. With an ungainly, awkward motion he swung his fist and punched David in the side of the head. The son staggered backwards over the graves.

"David!" Helen called. She caught him under the arms before he crashed to the ground.

"He hit me?"

"He doesn't know who you are. He's confused," Helen said.

David raised his hand to his chin. He could feel the impact of the blow on his jaw. It rattled the thoughts in his head, fracturing them so nothing made sense. "He hit me."

He turned back around. Leaning heavily on Helen. His legs felt like paper straws. Walking was impossible. He had to concentrate just to stay upright.

He heard the click of steel. Billy had clamped the bracelet from the handcuffs around one of Graham Chadwick's wrists. The second bracelet was hanging down, and when the dead man lashed out the metal circlet, it left a weal on Billy's face where it struck.

"Stop it, dad!"

The shout echoed across time. A sense of déjà vu.

Helen stepped past and pushed the dead man. Off balance, he slumped into the chair and Billy was able to close the loose bracelet from the handcuffs around the upright of the heavy wooden chair.

Graham Chadwick stood up, dragging the chair behind him. The weight only allowed him to move the chair a couple of centimetres and his arm stretched taut as if he was being pulled apart.

Billy pushed him into the seat.

"Sit *down!*" he shouted.

Graham Chadwick rocked on his heels before slumping into the seat. Billy glared at David over the head of the dead man. "Don't just stand there like a dummy. This is your gig."

It was like his thoughts were coated with mud. It was impossible to think straight. To move with purpose. David felt Helen's hand pull him forward, steering him around the open grave until he was standing in front of his father as the man wrestled to be free of the cuffs.

Billy glanced up at him. "You don't have long."

"What?" David asked.

"Until he's gone again. This time forever."

"What did you want to say to your father?" Helen asked.

David looked down at the man in the chair who

snarled and snapped as if he wanted to take a bite out of someone. He reached out with his free arm and formed a fist but Billy stood just beyond reach.

Trick me once . . . David thought to himself.

"This isn't my father," he said to Helen. It was so obvious. They'd made a mistake. The man on the chair might share a passing resemblance to the image on David's photograph—but the headstone lied. The man was twenty years in the ground, surely after that long, all bodies started to look the same—with sticks for arms and legs. A sunken face: no teeth, no eyes, no flesh to create features. Really the man was just a skull on top of a skeleton. He could be anyone.

"This is your father, David," Billy said to him. The words were soft but certain. "It has his name on the gravestone. They don't make mistakes."

"I don't recognise him," David said. It was a lie. Or at least the kernel of a lie. He stared at the man gnashing with his toothless gums and snapping his head around. He could have been anyone, that was true, but there was still something about the man which David found familiar.

"Talk to him," Helen suggested. "Maybe it will help him to calm down."

Billy shrugged at the suggestion. "Sometimes it makes a difference. Everyone responds to different things."

And some don't respond to anything, David thought. He was aware of Billy's earlier warning that a rising wasn't a time for family reunions. The stories in the newspaper of grandchildren weeping happily at the side of granny's grave as she told them one last story were the exceptions that warranted the media coverage.

"Dad?" David said.

The man cuffed to the chair didn't respond. David pushed away the sense of being ignored. He scrambled through his memory for anything from that period when his father had been alive—but he had been a small kid; how much did anyone remember from the time they were five? He had a couple of images in his head; a trip to Euro Disney with all the rides in primary colours; running out of school one day in winter when it fell like the snow was as tall as his thighs; checking under the pillow to see if the tooth fairy had visited. The memories were fragments, vague images and the memory of thoughts and feelings.

He tried to force himself to remember anything about his father. The scent of sweat when he came home from the factory. The way he used to brush his unshaven chin against his son's face. The thunder of his shout rolling through the house on a Saturday morning if David turned the television up too loud. The smell of cigarettes on his breath.

Did he smoke? The only photograph he had of his father gave no indication that the man smoked, but deep within the recesses of his memory, it felt like a truth: his father smoked, and shouted and stank of sweat when he came home from work in the evening.

"Graham Chadwick! Listen to your son!" Billy shouted like he was raising his voice to be understood by someone who was hard of hearing.

Maybe the worms are clogging up his ears, David thought. It reminded him of the times when he had visited his grandmother in the elderly persons' home and sat in the dayroom at visiting time, listening to visitors bawl at their relatives in order to be heard: *Did*

110

you have a nice night, Mum? Is your room warm enough? Do you need me to get you anything from the shops before I go?

The man trapped in the chair twisted his body. "Wharramarra?"

"This is your son, David." Billy took the man's chin in his hand, clamping the jaw shut so he could not bite him, and twisted his head around so he was pointed in David's direction. The act was hard, verging on brutal.

"Go easy!" Helen said.

"They can't feel anything," Billy said, speaking over the dead man's head. "That's why they're so dangerous. Pain doesn't stop them."

David wanted to believe his father was looking at him even though the dark orbits held nothing but grave dirt and spiders. He reached out his hand to touch his father, suppressing the instinct to shudder when he felt the cold, leathery skin beneath his fingertips.

"Are you okay, dad?"

The raw eye sockets of the dead man's skull peered into him.

David pushed away the disappointment. Billy had been right. His mother had been right. There was nothing to be gained from coming to the rising. No memories to be shared. No secrets to be revealed. His father had abandoned them and then he had died. That was the story. That was the whole story.

The dead man strained against the handcuffs. He lurched forward, raising the chair from the ground only for the weight to slam it back down into the earth.

"Lemmego."

David's heart stopped beating. There was

absolutely no doubt; his dad had spoken to him. He had looked directly at him and asked a question.

David took a step towards the chair.

"No!" Billy said.

"You heard him?"

"Yes. So I know you want to release him from those handcuffs. And I know that would be a bad idea."

The dead man in the chair wrestled against the fastening around his wrist. The motion scraped away the skin to expose the dirty-brown arm bones beneath.

"If he carries on like that he could break his wrist."

"I've not seen it happen. And I've witnessed clients a lot more powerful."

The flat, dispassionate tone of Billy's words was cold.

"He's not a client. He's my father."

The look Billy gave him suggested that was the sort of stupid thing a member of the family *would* say at a rising. David swung at the Family Director. He'd never been a distinguished fighter at school and now that inexperience came to the fore and his looping right hook missed Billy's jaw. His whole body followed the wild punch and he stumbled to remain on his feet. Billy didn't flinch. He looked almost bored.

David steadied himself to take a rush at the Family Director and pummel him into the ground. He was just a small thing. David would teach him to show respect to the dead. They weren't just clients who represented a source of income. They were people. Family.

He rushed forward.

Helen put herself in front of him as if she were protecting the little man in his trim black suit with the sweat patches spreading out across his dirty shirt. "Get out of the way," David said.

"You can't set your dad free. Look at him!"

David's first response was to push Helen aside so he could get at Billy. He put his hand on her shoulder.

"Look at him!" she insisted.

"Letmego!" Graham Chadwick shouted. He strained his muscles and once again the heavy chair lifted from the ground and then immediately fell back down, drilling four small holes into the dirt.

Billy picked up the camping chair and placed it directly in front of Graham Chadwick. "Sit," he said, and David felt Helen push him towards the chair, almost press him down into the seat.

He allowed himself to sink into the chair. The canvas webbing was lower than the wooden chair and so he looked up at his father, like a child peering up to his parent. He wondered whether Billy had intended this, or if it was simply a coincidence.

This close he could smell the dirt on his father's breath. He reached forward and touched the back of his dad's hand. "I'm sorry."

"Let me go," his dad said. The words were clear now. The empty skull bored its attention into David and he was five years old again. He stared up into his father's face and he no longer saw the raw bone of a skull twenty years in its grave, he saw the young man from the photograph, smiling for his new girlfriend.

"I can't."

"Let me fucking go!" his father shouted. He strained his arms and the metal links of the cuffs pulled taut. David realised he was afraid his father could break the cuffs, and given how angry he was, if his father broke them . . .

"No," Billy said. He positioned himself at the man's

side and pushed him back down into the chair. "You haven't got very long so you need to focus."

Graham Chadwick twisted his head to stare at the Family Director. "Fuck off!"

David wasn't sure why the swearing shocked him. It wasn't like he'd never used the occasional curse himself, and even his mother wasn't immune from letting out a stream of expletives if someone cut in front of her on the motorway. But from his father—the quiet, smiling man in the photograph—it felt wrong.

That sense of déjà vu returned. It was like looking at the photograph and seeing a second image underneath. One that was unfamiliar, but not entirely alien. The sensation drifted in like the stink of cigarette smoke on his father's breath or the stale taste of sweat at the back of his mouth each time he inhaled his father's aroma.

"You've only got a few minutes," Helen said.

The recognition terrified David. Helen was right. He sucked in a deep breath that dragged the scent of his father down to the bottom of his lungs, so he felt overwhelmed by the man's presence. He had a script. He'd actually written out exactly what to say when this moment came. The words were typed out and in one of the pockets of the bags that held the equipment behind the headstone of Graham Chadwick. They were words he had committed to memory. And they were gone. His mind buzzed with static.

"I'm sorry, dad."

He didn't even know why he was apologising. He wasn't responsible for whatever had happened to his father. He had been too young even to understand what was happening. His mother had driven him away. She never said so, but David knew from her guilt every time he tried to talk about his father that it had to be the case. Or at least that she felt she had driven him away.

"Why did you leave me?" David asked. The question was more brutal than he had intended, but he was aware of all the valuable minutes he had wasted trying to argue with Billy.

"Who are you?"

"Your son. David." He felt sick with the possibility that his father would claim no knowledge of him.

"David?"

He nodded in confirmation. Without eyes, without any real facial characteristics, it was impossible to read any emotion on the face of the man sitting opposite him, but David tried anyway. He wondered if he was watching confusion or remembrance.

"Spoilt brat," Graham Chadwick said. His mouth turned up in a sneer. "She rooned you."

Ruined? David wasn't sure if he understood what he was being told. His mother struggled financially throughout his childhood. She spent all her time apologising because he couldn't have computer games or the new clothes he coveted.

David considered hurrying to his bag to pull out the script he had written. Maybe something from the words he had carefully structured over the last twelve months could help him now.

"You haven't got long," Billy said. Behind the man's veneer of callous professionalism, David sensed genuine emotion; the Family Director was urging him to use the few minutes he had with his father.

"Mum doesn't know I'm here. She didn't want me to come."

"She wouldn't."

"Why?" David asked, but his father stared through him as if he wasn't really there.

"Why did you leave them?" Helen asked.

Graham Chadwick turned to face her. "WhoYou?" he slurred.

He's already going, David thought. Panic flooded through his system. How long did he have left? How many questions could he answer?

"I didn't leave," his father said.

"I remember . . . " David said and then stopped. There were a hundred things he wanted to ask but his own sentence stopped him dead. *I remember . . .*

What exactly *did* he remember?

Emotion throttled the breath in his throat. He was determined he wasn't going to cry. Not here. Not now. There would be time for that later. He dragged a thick gulp of air down into his lungs and pushed it out, asking the question again. "Why did you leave us?"

"I didn't leave." In the flat stillness of the cemetery, his father's words were as hard as a slap.

David looked to Billy for confirmation that the pent-up frustration and rage he was seeing infected all of the dead when they came to their rising. He searched the Family Director's face for reassurance but found none.

Graham Chadwick pulled his hand away from the chair. The metal bracelet cracked against the thin bones. His father's hand bent awkwardly. If it had been anyone else—anyone alive—they would have screamed in agony as the joints pulled apart.

"There's no point trying, it'll hold," Billy said. He turned and explained, "They're designed for exactly this scenario."

"Maybe, but then maybe dad has more anger built up in him than most," David said. He had a memory of cowering behind the settee as his father screamed at his mother. With the memory came the realisation that he no longer wanted to know why his father had left them. "No wonder she didn't want anyone at your rising," David said to the dead man. "She just wanted to forget you ever existed."

"She would," Graham Chadwick said. He pulled his arm away from the chair and when the bone finally snapped and the cuff released, he gave a shout of triumph and launched himself at David. His left arm still anchored him to the chair and prevented him from reaching his son with the haymaker of a punch he swung. Instead, he stumbled over the chair and crashed to his knees.

From the ground, he roared with rage and pulled himself into a standing position. He surged forward. The chair held solid. He pulled against it like a dog straining on a leash.

"There's no reason for this," Billy said in his authoritative voice.

Graham Chadwick swung at his son. When the punch fell short he put all his attention into straining the cuff which fixed him to the chair.

"You'll just break both of your wrists," Billy said, but David thought he detected concern in the Family Director's words as if he recognised it was possible the dead man could break free entirely.

The wooden chair creaked with the strain.

They don't feel pain, Billy had said, *that's what makes them so dangerous*. Now David understood what he meant. It was like watching a bear gnawing its own leg to escape a trap. "Why don't you just die?" David shouted.

Now as the man raged, David was overwhelmed with terror. What would happen if his father was able to free himself from the chair? *When* his father freed himself from the chair because that now seemed inevitable. He wished he had something as solid and simple as a baseball bat to protect himself and Helen.

His list of questions was gone. He no longer needed to know what had happened. He no longer *wanted* to know.

He took a step away from the grave and looked behind him. They could lock themselves in the truck, or even drive away and wait an hour or two until it was safe and then they could come back and rebury his father.

The more his father raged against the handcuff which fastened him to the chair, the more certain David was that he didn't want to be around when his father freed himself.

He held out a hand to Helen, but he couldn't do it. He couldn't abandon his father.

The man howled like a tortured animal. David wanted to clamp his hands over his ears to block out the sound but refused to do so. Everyone had told him not to do this—Helen, his mother, the Family Directors, Billy, even Nathaniel; they had all warned him about getting involved in his father's rising. But he was stubborn and arrogant and this was the price.

"Hand me the Heelan cutters," Billy shouted at him.

David couldn't move.

The joints of the chair creaked. Creaked again. And then snapped.

CHAPTER 16

GRAHAM CHADWICK LAUNCHED himself at David. He covered the distance in a fraction of a second, too fast for David to react. The dead man was upon him, the sharp stub of his broken wrist scratching against David's chest while he tried to claw at him with his left hand. His jaws worked hard, snapping empty gums together. Between howls of rage, he emitted a high-pitched squeal.

David tried to push his father away, but the man was too strong. David felt the hard edge of the gravestone press into the back of his knees and he understood he had nowhere left to retreat.

He sensed Helen trying to claw his father away from him.

"Leave him alone!" she shouted. At first, David was unsure who she was shouting at.

"He's your son! Don't you understand?"

The words rippled. Like a stone dropped into water. Waves pushing backwards through time. David stared into the dark cavities that had once held his father's eyes and knew his father understood he was attacking his son.

He put his hands on his father's chest to push him

away and felt ribs against his palms. It was like pressing the bars of a cage.

Hot blood ran down his chin. His father swung his left hand in a clumsy swipe which missed David, only for the metal bracelet of the handcuff to hit him on the temple. He tried to blink away the pain that felt like a crease inside his brain.

He punched his father. His knuckles scraped bone. The sound of the man's jaws clattering together ran through David's nerves.

Graham Chadwick pushed forward again, ignorant of the punch. He flailed at David with his left hand and right arm.

David was struck in the face. He was scratched across the throat. His breath stopped for a moment. He was punched in the stomach. Kicked. Gouged. Bitten.

He slapped at his father. He lifted his hands in front of his face and when that didn't protect him, he started to punch the man in his chest to keep him away. He grabbed the lapels of his father's dusty jacket and the old cloth ripped along the seams leaving David holding a handful of black wool. The next time he grabbed at his father the jacket parted in two.

His father's shirt was grey rather than white. There were yellow stains on the material. Threadbare patches showed through to the grey-green skin beneath.

His father came forward again. David pushed him back and bought himself a few seconds of breathing space.

The dead man gouged a scratch along David's arm. He squealed in surprise and pain and then looked down as the blood bloomed across his shirt.

Somewhere under that mess was his arm. God alone knew what sort of infections he might catch.

He slapped at the man but it had no effect. Graham Chadwick attacked again. David stepped back and fell over the concrete border at the edge of the grave. He slammed into the ground. The impact clattered together the teeth in his head.

The dead man fell upon him, fingers ripping at the skin around his throat. Jawbones snapping together. His father punched him in the stomach and the air fled from David's body. He felt a rib crack. For the first time it occurred to David that he could be seriously hurt. He could be killed.

He tried to push his father away from him. The man weighed nothing but still clawed at him. Punched him. Bit him. David was overwhelmed by the presence of the dead man. He kicked him in the groin but it made no difference. The dead man continued to attack.

Graham Chadwick punched his son in the chest, and David felt the heat of the wound as the man's jagged finger bones pierced his skin, scraped between his ribs, and slipped into his lung.

David screamed with pain, white hot and ice cold at the same time. His scream immediately faded to a whisper. When he tried to cry out all he heard escape his lips was the soft whistle of air.

The world faded to grey, and then black. David bit down on his own lips and the pain brought him back to consciousness but he could feel himself slipping away again.

The heavy crunch of metal against bone sounded distant. Immediately the pressure of the hand buried in his chest slackened. The world remained shades of grey, but now he could focus on the shapes around him. He saw Helen standing above him, still holding the spade she had used to club Graham Chadwick. She stood, watching the dead man, waiting to see if she needed to hit him again.

The image was familiar.

CHAPTER 17

DAVID LAY AT the side of the grave and watched as Helen and Billy returned his father to the grave and began to pile dirt over his dead body. Each time he breathed in, a stabbing pain rushed into his chest. When he breathed out his vision flickered from grey to black.

"Are you okay?" Helen asked.

He nodded. It was the only response he could give. Helen repeated her earlier promise, "The ambulance will be here soon." It felt like she had been saying the same line forever, that he was trapped in a world where they were always re-burying his father and the ambulance would never arrive.

He didn't think he was going to die. Billy had looked at him and proclaimed that he had seen worse injuries.

"In the early days I saw a rising in which three of the family had been gored by the dead relative. Not one of mine: I was dealing with my own client elsewhere in the cemetery."

Helen's face was covered with dirt from the grave. Her hair was matted with clumps of mud. Rats-tails draped across her shoulders.

Billy stepped into his line of sight. He wore a bleached-clean shirt and even his tie was perfectly black. His shoes looked like they had been wiped but still retained a few traces of mud. "Your father's gone." He spoke without any emotion—just another professional assessment of a job completed.

"Thanks," David managed to say.

Billy opened his mouth as if he was going to say something else. Maybe to make the point that amateurs only put themselves and everyone else in danger. He put his hand into his pocket and David wondered whether he was going to be presented with a bill for the work.

He closed his eyes and nausea overwhelmed him like a crashing wave. He heard again the heavy thud of the spade as it connected with the back of his father's head.

A sound that once he had heard it, he would have assumed he could never forget.

"Your mother?" Helen asked.

David nodded his head. The movement caused the muscles in his neck to spasm, and nausea rushed to take another pass through his system. "She doesn't need to know."

Helen nodded.

David closed his eyes. "I'm going to be sick," he muttered, but the idea of vomiting on the grave, even the grave of his wifebeater of a father, was enough to force him to swallow down the bile that rose up in his throat.

He heard the crunch of the ambulance tyres as the vehicle rolled into the car park. It still felt like something happening a million miles away to someone who was not David Chadwick. Another person. Someone who had attended his father's rising.

He closed his eyes. Listened to the cemetery.

THE END?

Not if you want to dive into more of Crystal Lake Publishing's Tales from the Darkest Depths!

Check out our amazing website and online store.
https://www.crystallakepub.com

We always have great new projects and content on the website to dive into, as well as a newsletter, behind the scenes options, social media platforms, our own dark fiction shared-world series and our very own webstore. If you use the IGotMyCLPBook! coupon code in the store (at the checkout), you'll get a one-time-only 50% discount on your first eBook purchase!

Our webstore even has categories specifically for KU books, non-fiction, anthologies, and of course more novels and novellas.

ABOUT THE AUTHOR

Richard Farren Barber was born in Nottingham in July 1970. After studying in London he returned to the East Midlands. He lives with his wife and son and works as a manager for a local university. He's fairly confident people only read these bios to check the author isn't a serial killer (spoiler alert: he's not.)!

He has over 80 short stories published, as well as seven novellas: *The Power of Nothing*; *The Sleeping Dead*; *Odette*; *Perfect Darkness, Perfect Silence*; *Closer Still*; *All Hell*, and *Twenty Years Dead*. His two novels are *The Living and the Lost* and *The Screaming Dead* (co-authored with Peter Mark May).

If you want to check on his serial killer tendencies, follow him on twitter.com/rfarrenbarber and www.facebook.com/richardfarrenbarber

His website can be found here: www.richardfarrenbarber.co.uk

"Bayou Whispers *is a haunting, touching novel that blends the horrors of everyday life with that of the supernatural. Tapping into the tension and setting of films like* Angel Heart *and* True Detective*, this is a hypnotic story told from a place of loss, community, and resolute hope.*"
- Richard Thomas

Readers . . .

Thank you for reading *Twenty Years Dead*. We hope you enjoyed this novella.

If you have a moment, please review *Twenty Years Dead* at the store where you bought it.

Help other readers by telling them why you enjoyed this book. No need to write an in-depth discussion. Even a single sentence will be greatly appreciated. Reviews go a long way to helping a book sell, and is great for an author's career. It'll also help us to continue publishing quality books. You can also share a photo of yourself holding this book with the hashtag #IGotMyCLPBook!

Thank you again for taking the time to journey with Crystal Lake Publishing.

Visit our Linktree page for a list of our social media platforms. https://linktr.ee/CrystalLakePublishing

Folk horror at its most cosmic and terrifying.

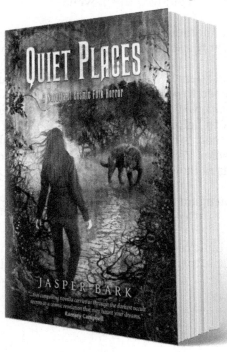

"A heady mix of folk horror and the psychological, of religious yearning and the uncannily atavistic, this compelling novella carries us through the darkest occult secrets to a cosmic revelation that may haunt your dreams." **- Ramsey Campbell**

Our Mission Statement:

Since its founding in August 2012, Crystal Lake Publishing has quickly become one of the world's leading publishers of Dark Fiction and Horror books in print, eBook, and audio formats.

While we strive to present only the highest quality fiction and entertainment, we also endeavour to support authors along their writing journey. We offer our time and experience in non-fiction projects, as well as author mentoring and services, at competitive prices.

With several Bram Stoker Award wins and many other wins and nominations (including the HWA's Specialty Press Award), Crystal Lake Publishing puts integrity, honor, and respect at the forefront of our publishing operations.

We strive for each book and outreach program we spearhead to not only entertain and touch or comment on issues that affect our readers, but also to strengthen and support the Dark Fiction field and its authors.

Not only do we find and publish authors we believe are destined for greatness, but we strive to work with men and woman who endeavour to be decent human beings who care more for others than themselves, while still being hard working, driven, and passionate artists and storytellers.

Crystal Lake Publishing is and will always be a beacon of what passion and dedication, combined with overwhelming teamwork and respect, can accomplish. We endeavour to know each and every one of our readers, while building personal relationships with our authors, reviewers, bloggers, podcasters, bookstores, and libraries.

We will be as trustworthy, forthright, and transparent as any business can be, while also keeping most of the headaches away from our authors, since it's our job to solve the problems so they can stay in a creative mind. Which of course also means paying our authors.

We do not just publish books, we present to you worlds within your world, doors within your mind, from talented authors who sacrifice so much for a moment of your time.

There are some amazing small presses out there, and through collaboration and open forums we will continue to support other presses in the goal of helping authors and showing the world what quality small presses are capable of accomplishing. No one wins when a small press goes down, so we will always be there to support hardworking, legitimate presses and their authors. We don't see Crystal Lake as the best press out there, but we will always strive to be the best, strive to be the most interactive and grateful, and even blessed press around. No matter what happens over time, we will also take our mission very seriously while appreciating where we are and enjoying the journey.

What do we offer our authors that they can't do for themselves through self-publishing?

We are big supporters of self-publishing (especially hybrid publishing), if done with care, patience, and planning. However, not every author has the time or inclination to do market research, advertise, and set up book launch strategies. Although a lot of authors are successful in doing it all, strong small presses will always be there for the authors who just want to do what they do best: write.

What we offer is experience, industry knowledge, contacts and trust built up over years. And due to our strong brand and trusting fanbase, every Crystal Lake Publishing book comes with weight of respect. In time our fans begin to trust our judgment and will try a new author purely based on our support of said author.

With each launch we strive to fine-tune our approach, learn from our mistakes, and increase our reach. We continue to assure our authors that we're here for them and that we'll carry the weight of the launch and dealing with third parties while they focus on their strengths—be it writing, interviews, blogs, signings, etc.

We also offer several mentoring packages to authors that include knowledge and skills they can use in both traditional and self-publishing endeavours.

We look forward to launching many new careers.

This is what we believe in. What we stand for. This will be our legacy.

Welcome to Crystal Lake Publishing— Tales from the Darkest Depths.

Made in the USA
Middletown, DE
30 May 2022

66401875R00080